Lesson Learned

An
Agent Carrie Harris
Action Thriller

G J Stevens

Copyright © GJ Stevens 2012-2020

The moral right of GJ Stevens to be identified as the author of this work has been asserted by him in accordance with the Copyright, Designs, and Patents Act 1998.

British Library Cataloguing-in-Publication Data
A catalogue record for this book is available from the British Library

Cover Illustration Copyright © 2020 by Gareth Stevens
Cover design by Jessica Bell Design

ISBN: 9798629589051

Other Books by GJ Stevens

Agent Carrie Harris Action Thrillers

OPERATION DAWN WOLF
CAPITAL ACTION
THE GEMINI ASSIGNMENT

James Fisher Series

FATE'S AMBITION

Post-apocalyptic Thrillers

IN THE END
BEFORE THE END
AFTER THE END
BEGINNING OF THE END

SURVIVOR – Your Guide to Surviving the Apocalypse

DEDICATION

To the men and woman who tirelessly work to make our world a safer place, putting themselves in harm's way so we can sleep soundly.

ACKNOWLEDGMENTS

Thanks to all those who helped me along the way, be it big or small, I am grateful.

Have you read Capital Action?

If not, then grab your free copy by joining my mailing list.

Get your free copy at www.gjstevens.com

1

Closing the message window and clicking the default icon just in time, I gazed at Celina's slender feet as she descended the stairs into the open-plan living room. Turning in the swivel chair, I peered to my right, still watching as she walked past the front door near the foot of the stairs and across the room before balancing herself on the edge of the armchair opposite.

All this whilst I listened to the hard disk's gentle rattle, confirming the script hurriedly searched out all trace of my keypresses and messages sent and received in the last half an hour, replacing at furious speed with a benign digital footprint.

"Good morning Catarina. Couldn't you sleep?" she said, her soft, accented voice croaky as if she'd just woken.

I tried not to stare at the lace edges of her night clothes, just visible through the thin silk gown draped over her shoulders.

"No," I said, pulling my towelling robe tight around my chest in an effort to hide my cleavage. "I thought I'd email my sister before I get on with the day. She worries about me."

"I bet she does. I would too if you were my sister and had just turned twenty-one, then headed to a foreign land to become an au pair. I'd imagine all the new people you'd meet and the exciting experiences you'd have," she said, laughing as she swept her long blonde hair behind her ears. "How's that going for you?"

I gave a one-sided smile.

"Can I get you a coffee?" I asked.

"You carry on," she replied, nodding towards the computer.

"It's fine. I'm done," I said, standing and arranging my robe for the second time.

"Okay then."

"And for Mr Rozman?" I asked as I took a step through the doorway leading to the dining room.

"No. You should know by now my husband doesn't like to wake before the sun at the weekend," she said with a grin which seemed a little forced on her sleep-puffed face.

It had nothing to do with the bottle of whiskey I clear away each Saturday morning. I didn't voice the thought as I headed to the kitchen, leaving Celina curling her feet under herself in the armchair, her hands spreading the thin gown across her legs.

Refilling filter paper, coffee grounds and water, I couldn't help but again wonder why someone so young — she couldn't have been more than five years older than me — would marry a man in his late fifties and take on his two teenage kids.

He didn't live like a rich man, despite the large house in the suburbs and her active social life. Perhaps it was their shared nationality, both foreigners in this land; giving each other a level of understanding they wouldn't get from a native.

With ash blonde hair running down her back, blue eyes which made me think there should be a deeper meaning to her life other than her duty to him upstairs, and long, pin-straight legs, she was way above his grade.

With a pug-face and rotund belly, he worked all hours, barely appearing during the week, then spending most of the weekend in bed whilst seeming to insist she be at his side when he woke. He never bothered to hide his furious grunts from travelling across the house as he climbed on top of her.

Perhaps she pitied him.

His first wife had died five years ago in a horrific fire which destroyed his last home. The children were away at their aunt's. He was on his way home for the candlelit dinner which caused the tragic blaze.

At first, Celina had seemed happy enough, but as my first few weeks with the family passed by, her loneliness became obvious. She insisted on employing the hired help; not only myself, but the part-time gardener, too, to manage the grounds which were fifty-times bigger than the house. All kept perfectly manicured. Each blown leaf picked up the next morning. Each blade of grass shorn back at the first sign of growth.

The gardener was a tall native of the small town. His tanned, leathered skin pulled tight with a constant smile and with arms like tree trunks, I could see why Celina had handpicked him for the task.

Lenart Rozman must be weak, or lazy enough not to care. Or too stupid to know what he signed off.

For my first few days, Celina would follow me around the house. Talking about nothing much, she would watch me work, slowing me enough that Lenart noticed my tasks were either incomplete or below his standard. She'd backed off when the threat of my dismissal became serious.

Now we just caught up on the odd moment when the house was quiet and I'd finished my tasks, until the kids had the chance to wake and turn it upside down again.

All the talk came from her, the same as always. With her hands wrapped around the coffee mug, she'd told me about the bore of a new tennis partner the club had assigned her; a lady of sixty, or thereabouts. Spritely enough to keep up, although with the conversation of someone a generation above, it just made Celina's afternoons at that place even more of a chore.

I'd long given up asking why she went. I knew Lenart was the reason. The women's tennis club, in his eyes, was the perfect place for a restless young wife to spend her days out of temptation's way.

Celina had been my first focus.

A young, blonde wife with a blemish-free face. White teeth. Flat stomach and bouncy tits. All lonely in the suburbs while her husband worked long hours in the city. It would be her face in the manual, if they'd ever printed one.

The gardener was the second; bait for the lonely housewife. Large garden, just enough work, but not too much; a bit of neglect wouldn't get noticed.

I'd seen them together many times; their manner friendly, but no more flirty than you'd expect. They weren't having an affair. Yet. I knew from the washing the only action she was getting was on the husband's long weekend lay-ins.

I considered the children outsiders to the process, but I hadn't ruled them out.

Lenart was the next focus, although I had very few dealings with him. He'd been in on the interview, his face lightening as he saw me; his nods as Celina looked to confirm her decision on the spot. Since then, we'd only seen one another in company, with Celina at his side or the children running around or screaming some injustice the way they do at that important age.

It intrigued me as to how he'd react if we were ever alone. I hoped to discover who he was; what he was about.

All I could figure so far were the few cursory words Celina had spoken about him. I hadn't ruled out that those words could be the depth of her knowledge.

He worked in high finance; company money. Investments and other such broad terms. The company wasn't his, rather some multinational whose aim was to shuffle currency this way and that.

That's where I should have left it.

My instructions were to settle in and become a part of the family; an efficient au pair taking the lion's share of the chores and the childcare. I could only listen and get to know them; investigation strictly prohibited.

I had no idea of my ultimate purpose. Maybe I'd never know. I could be out of here tomorrow, next week, next year, or given a command to execute within a few moments. To take something. Someone. Their life or to unearth their secrets. But so far, the coded messages read the same each week, despite my probing:

Instructions:

Observe. Report.

2

At first I did exactly as asked, reporting my findings in efficient paragraphs detailing the facts; a few lines for each of the family, describing their activities during the week.

By the fourth week, I realised each report contained pretty much the same information. A quick copy and paste would have given the same effect.

No change from last week, and the one before that.

At the start of the sixth, I decided to give the house a deep clean. The decision had nothing to do with the new pace of life being too slow compared to the frantic chaos of the last twelve months of selection and training.

On Monday morning I told Celina about my plans. She told me she'd love to help but couldn't as she'd already decided to spend the day in the city, shopping for the upcoming Christmas holidays. I didn't remind her they were three months away to the day.

As the house emptied, I started at the top, sprinkling cleaning materials around the landing. Spraying polish in the air and with a duster tucked into my jeans pocket, I took to the marital bedroom.

No investigation. Just cleaning.

As I ran the cloth over dust-free surfaces, I found no secret compartments buried in the walls. No loose carpet at the edges. No safe in the floorboards. Nothing stashed in the cupboards in their ensuite.

I found his dusty, dog-eared porn collection; long ago boxed away, the pages faded.

I found her sex toys in her bottom drawer of her bedside table, shielded only by a small towel. No dust had settled. He clearly wasn't enough for her.

The whole house took the day and much of my energy. There were no documents, save for ancient payslips, the house and car insurance, diligent car service invoices and checklists, repairs and bills. All laid out so neat and tidy. Nothing marked Top Secret.

Everything I found backed up their stories. The house was completely clean, free of dirt and my interest.

I left it another few days, burying my head into the work. It had become clear that whatever I'd been sent here to observe was not in this house. After all, why else would they let me, a stranger, have free roam?

I had use of a car; a little Fiesta for shopping and errands, but not on my one day off a week, which was still a few days away. Stepping out of the front door, which I'd done very little of these last few weeks, I took in the sight of the thin line of houses, double the amount lining the side we were on. My current home was the only one of two on this side of the road; the other, a few paces away, sat full of builders who banged and clattered all day long, with deliveries coming late into the night.

The neighbours had moved out, the remodelling underway ever since I'd been on the scene.

The estate, Celina had told me, had been originally built for the workers of the chemical factory which sat a short distance behind the houses, sold over ten years earlier when the chemicals market depressed. From miles around you could still see the single tall chimney looking as if rising from a forest of tall, stocky trees. A thin continual column of white smoke made it visible for miles around.

Taking in the breath of forest air, I took the car, stopping part way to the supermarket and heading down a deserted track. For the next half an hour I roamed over and under its metal, inside and out, but found nothing to show any device tracking its movement.

Still, I had a story ready; the dirt track was halfway up a hill and offered great views to the otherwise flat brown land spreading out at my feet.

The rest of the journey to the supermarket took me along a narrow road which seemed to have been built to some imaginary constraints, making only minimal use of the wide sprawling dusty ground either side. In places it was so thin I had to pull onto the dirt when anything bigger than a car headed from the opposite direction. I'd often slow to a crawl as a coach or a lorry forged its way past me.

With no clear reason, the developers had built the supermarket in the middle of nowhere. A twenty-minute drive from the estate, the squat building sprawled across a massive area behind a vast car park, which I'd never seen more than a third full, if that. The road continued, disappearing to the horizon and not touching civilisation until it joined the interstate after another fifty miles.

 The only companion to the supermarket was a diner guarding the entrance to the car park. Each time I'd visit, coaches would nestle around the building and I'd pause for a moment to watch the passengers coming and going.

I'd stare on with intrigue as large parties of kids or disabled people or foreign tourists with cameras shuffled from the building. Groups of women seemed to be popular; I could only guess at some local attraction I hadn't yet heard of pulling in charities from around the nearest towns.

The chemical factory was the only destination I knew to be around, but I'd only been here a few weeks. The coaches were always parked facing the direction I'd come from. Not the other way around; seeming to never stop on the return journey, which I guessed would make sense if the destination were local.

I made a mental note to take a coffee in the diner and find out about what drew them in. Maybe it would be worth a visit when I let myself have a few moments downtime.

After the supermarket, I detoured past the house, visiting a short strip mall and stocking up on envelopes and writing paper of a quality I knew I could only get this side of the house. I paid with cash, not the family's credit card meant only for the weekly shop.

After another short detour, I rolled past the entrance to the Country Club, my gaze lingering on Celina's small Mercedes parked at the grand palm-surrounded building.

At home I'd barely put the shopping away before Celina, still in her short tennis skirt and white tank top, followed me through the door two hours earlier than normal. She lingered in the kitchen doorway, watching me thumb through a cook book with a thin sheen of moisture still covering her skin.

She explained she'd had enough of dried up old ladies for the day and was dying for some conversation with someone who had something interesting to say.

"It's a shame you don't play tennis," she said as I tried not to look up from the book.

"I do," I replied, "but this place keeps me busy."

Celina laughed and I watched her bare feet out of the corner of my eye as she took a few steps towards me. Still thumbing through the book, I could smell from the salt and faint tang of alcohol she'd drawn close.

Listening to the control in her breath, I turned. "I have to prepare dinner."

She stood closer than I thought, her head nearly at my shoulder. With a wide smile, she shook her head.

"I'll be in the shower if you need me," she said and turned to leave.

Hearing her footsteps up the stairs, I took an involuntary deep breath. I turned the book over, saving the page and headed up the steps with my feet at either edge to dull its creak. Standing at her wide-open door, I saw her tennis clothes in a pile on the floor to the sound of the shower hissing in the ensuite with its door half open.

Lingering for a moment, I gazed at the beige of her outline in the misted glass. Turning to leave I heard her pleasure, my gaze settling on the bottom drawer of her bedside table and the towel cast to the side.

I hurried down the stairs and began furiously chopping vegetables, forcing thoughts out of my mind and pushing away ideas that could impede my task.

Celina came down within half an hour, her face red, skin pink, breastbone flushed scarlet against the white of a low-cut top.

"You didn't need me then?" she said from the

doorway.

"No. I have everything I need."

"So do I," she said with a flutter of laughter. "You do too much for us. You're only supposed to be helping. A gap year is meant to be about exploring the culture." She paused. "I should have advised you against this place. There's nothing like that here."

"I like the work," I replied. "And this place is okay."

"You don't want okay. You need wow. You need to be out there doing new things. Experimenting with life. Finding yourself."

"Did you find yourself?"

She laughed again, but it soon drained to silence.

"No. Life found me."

"What do you mean?" I replied as I stopped chopping and turned towards her.

"Nothing, sorry. I'm taking up your time again."

A knock rattled against the front door and Celina turned with a start to greet the visitor but came back to the kitchen within a few minutes with a smile replacing the void she'd left with.

"They're back," she announced with a great excitement.

"Who?"

"The Bukia's at fifty-six and they have an au pair now. Isn't that exciting?" she said, her eyes wide.

Celina was off the list, or at least greyed out. For now.

3

Celina's daily trips to the tennis club got shorter. At the end of the following week she'd left the house for just an hour as if showing up just to be counted, then heading home when she wouldn't be missed by her partner who was likely asleep in a comfy armchair.

I suspected her comings and goings had synchronised with my schedule of shopping and errands.

She was either monitoring me, her trust faltering when she realised I'd been over their home with a fine-toothed comb, or she was trying to get me into bed. Her persistent actions spoke volumes as to which one it was.

After arriving home, Celina would seek me out and announce she was showering, often calling me to her room, shouting from the ensuite with some excuse; a forgotten towel or empty bottle of shampoo.

Each time I arrived she would be in some state of undress, more flesh on show on every new occasion as if her need grew more urgent.

Often she'd leave her drawer open with the small towel discarded to the side to show off its contents. Sometimes the long round edges of the pleasure tools would be on display across the bed.

After the shower, and dressed in thin, silk nightwear or just a towelling gown, she'd hang around as I busied myself with the chores.

I remained strong, despite the distraction, telling myself I had to keep removed, despite her advances. And they were distracting, leading to many frustrated nights and not just because her increased appearance hampered the investigations I shouldn't be conducting.

At one stage I thought her approach could be a tactic deployed to overcome me. We'd covered seduction in training, but only as a technique to use on our targets. No one mentioned how we should deal with it when used as a weapon towards us.

Of course, she could just be lonely, or perhaps she had a thing for strawberry blondes.

Either way, the best I could do was to keep her at bay without closing her off, storing the opportunity for later if it gave me an advantage in achieving a future goal.

I paused at the thought. Would I do the same if she were a man?

Two weeks into what seemed to have turned into a concerted campaign, I told her I was heading into the city. Celina offered to come with me, reducing the offer to a lift as she read the response I couldn't hide from my features.

In the end I decided I would postpone the trip, her face lifting when I took up the earlier offer of tennis. The club was somewhere I hadn't been inside and I wanted to see what she got up to. Observation only.

Later that day, we stepped into the foyer, both of us dressed in a tight skirt and vest top, mine a match she'd insisted I borrow. It took only seconds for me to agree it was a truly uninspiring place. She'd been right about the clientele too.

Of the handful of women I saw, each were all middle-aged or more. The only men were young, overly attentive waiters swarming around the lounges in dinner jackets and ties, doing a poor job of hiding their real intent which seemed to be to find a sugar mummy.

Deflecting their advances, we spent the next couple of hours on court. It was the first real moment of the assignment I'd enjoyed.

Celina was a mean opponent, bouncing around the court, her energy taking me by surprise. She must have been spending at least some of her time on the court. I hadn't played since school, but I could react and power the shots like I'd been playing all my life. Still I let her win, but only just.

Skipping the showers we stopped for a glass of wine in the lounge, the place no busier or quieter than when we'd arrived. The waiters soon got the idea we weren't interested in what they offered and we got down to chat, steering clear of subjects centring around the house and the family.

She began by delving into my back story, its detail not tested since the interview so many weeks ago now, but keeping the conversation light I had no trouble in keeping to the script.

***

Arriving home, she dragged me by the hand to the kitchen, pouring two glasses of wine and pinching the rest of the bottle under her arm as she led me to the garden.

On the cushion-covered rattan sofa she quizzed my thoughts of Brad, the gardener, as we watched him bare-chested, his biceps tensing as he dug over the vegetable patch. She told how she'd engineered his employment and not for his horticultural skills, adding it was lucky he was so cheap or Lenart might have put up a fight.

I asked her outright if she would ever have an affair. She sniggered, not denying it, just saying she wouldn't rule out a bit of fun with the hired help. Turning away, I felt her gaze continue to bore into my side as she spoke whilst I poured the last contents of my glass down my throat, realising it was going down much quicker than I'd expected.

I was storing up a problem for later in the day, but I just needed to keep it together for the next hour until the children came home.

Changing the subject to her husband, I hoped the conversation would steer her thought away or dampen her mood, but she brushed it aside.

She had no animosity towards him, but was brazen in her disregard for how their relationship might be affected if she strayed.

Celina switched the subject again, this time redirecting the enquiry to my past boyfriends, or girlfriends, or both, to use her exact words. She was more than a little taken aback when I told her the truth that I had no experience with either.

The shock in her expression only just matched the

undercurrent of excitement. A sudden fear hit me she'd scrunch up her face and pinch at my cheeks.

Emptying the bottle into each of the glasses, she turned to the side, waving as Brad put his hand up in our direction with his top back in place. He'd finished for the day. Now we were alone and in the sprawling garden we may as well have been in the middle of nowhere.

I checked my watch, only minutes to go.

"Well I better shower and get the dinner ready," I said. "The children will be back soon."

I watched as she held back words she seemed desperate to voice, closing her mouth before she could make a sound.

4

The restless night that followed helped me focus, forging my resolve. I wouldn't get into that situation again unless my assignment required the result.

I worried I'd already lost my way, distracted by her pretty face and the simple thoughts she seemed to force into my brain.

Although I shouldn't have been investigating, simple observation my explicit instruction, I was still a long way from crossing the husband off the list.

The next day, a Tuesday, was always set aside for shopping. I rattled through my chores, leaving the house before Celina could get me alone after avoiding her attempts to lock eyes over the breakfast table.

Out in the driveway I watched a woman not too far from my age, with long brown hair running down below her shoulders, leave the house next door, the house only reoccupied the week before after the builders had finished. She spotted me and waved in my direction.

I guessed she was their me, in one way at least. I waved back and couldn't help watching out of the corner of my eye as we both climbed into our cars.

After following her to the squat supermarket, I was sure she hadn't noticed me right at her tail for the entire journey, or so her surprise read as I parked at her side in the large car park. After regarding me with her brow furrowed, we broke into laughter and our hands descended to shake before swapping introductions.

She was Alarica, from Berlin, although her accent could well have been native. She'd been in the country for four years studying.

For now I was Catarina from just outside London.

She spoke perfect English. I quipped my German was basic, but surprised her as we continued the conversation in her native tongue. I was, after all, on a gap year following my studies, a recent language graduate.

She was on a journey to find herself, she said, laughing, soon admitting she had no idea what that meant. She'd been with the Bukia's since they'd moved out from the city an hour away; three months now.

She was a helping hand to the family, the mother unable to do all she needed to run the busy house. Alarica was part cleaner, part carer, part mother and part chauffeur. The father of the family didn't drive. He had a driver, but sometimes he wasn't around.

We chatted as we walked, picking from the shelves, switching to English when the stares of the natives fell in our direction. She told of the kindness from the family and how the parents and the children got along so well.

I told her I was yet to grow a strong bond with mine. It was still early days, but they were very nice, letting slip that I hardly ever saw the father and the children, their lives too busy. Celina, however, was always around and keen for company.

"Too keen?" Alarica said with a smile across the shelves. I let a small grin escape as my reply. "I've got a lot of friends in this business and it happens. More than you'd think. I bet no-one told you that before you signed up?"

"No," I replied, busying myself with bright boxes of breakfast cereal.

"It's the dads or the sons most of the time, but the wives do it, too. Especially when they're not the mother."

"Step mum," I said, nodding and Alarica replied with a smile. "What about you?"

"Never happened, and this is my second family. I don't think I've the attributes."

I laughed as I looked over her plump tits, lingering on the full lips telling the lie.

Alarica laughed along, realising the obvious. I could already see her confidence coming through; she couldn't hide those tells. A tinge to her smile, that look away at a key moment. I'd known her for only ten minutes, but each of her words, each movement of her body, calibrated my natural senses.

She was sleeping with the father, or the mother; which one wasn't clear. The father was the more likely and in a few more conversations it would be as obvious as if she'd stamped it across her forehead.

We split after the extended trip, adding a coffee in the diner and proposing a catch up on her day off. She had two each week and told me I should speak to my family about getting the same. We agreed we'd sort something in the next few weeks, but she mentioned we'd catch up at the party at the weekend.

"Oh, haven't they told you about it?" she said at my stone-faced response.

"No," I replied. "They probably just forgot."

"Lenara, that's Mrs Bukia, said you were more than welcome."

"I'm sure they'll mention it," I said. We left it at that.

Arriving home, the meeting had muddled my day. I'd planned to be out of the house, finding any errands until I could leave it late to come home. Realising only as I pulled up in the empty drive, I waved goodbye to Alarica as she headed into her house.

I took the shopping into the kitchen without even thinking about when I'd need to put my guard up. Celina would be at the club and I hoped she'd resume her normal routine.

Those thoughts dashed as I heard a car roll up the driveway. It was her, dressed in tennis whites but with no sheen of sweat; instead, like a homing missile she found me in the larder loading the cupboards.

"I didn't get a chance to speak with you this morning," she said, standing in the doorway, her voice sounding wounded. "Were you avoiding me?"

"Of course not," I replied, trying not to catch her gaze. "I just wanted to get the shopping done early."

"Great. That means we've got the rest of the day to ourselves, and we're all invited to a party next door at the weekend."

"Oh, but won't I just get in the way?"

"No. Lenart is on a trip with some chums, so you can be my date."

I coughed into my fist, hurrying to push away the cartons of juice.

"You could take Brad. He'd look so much better on your arm."

"A little obvious, don't you think? Who takes the gardener to a house warming?" She paused and gave a little laugh. "I could invite you both. That would make an interesting evening." She paused again.

I didn't look up, but I knew she was trying to gauge my reaction and she soon broke into laughter, which sounded more than a little forced. "That would be silly, yes. You'll come though, won't you?"

"What about the children?"

"They could come too, but that might spoil the night. No, I'll arrange for them to stay with friends. This will be so much fun."

I had no out. She'd taken them all away. Although I wouldn't be working all the time, I couldn't say no. Plus it might be an idea to get to know the neighbours, I told myself.

"Okay, I'll come," I replied and went back to being busy in the cupboards.

"Great," she said. "I'm off for a shower. Come up as soon as you're ready and you can help me choose what to wear."

5

My observation reports grew as I summarised the ongoing saga with Celina.

I left out irrelevant details, like the challenges I faced. I didn't mention how I had to hold myself back as she spent an hour undressing whilst I sat in her bedroom chair, each dress or skirt or blouse requiring different knickers, a different bra. The changes made in the orbit of my personal space so I could be under no illusion how much she enjoyed herself.

When she insisted I try clothes on too, I left to dress in my small room, trying each on and only returning to twirl for her amusement in the long dress I'd chosen for how much of my body wasn't on show.

She didn't hide her disappointment when I chose a skirt which stopped just at my ankles. I picked long sleeves covering even my wrists, a collar buttoned tight under my chin; the fit loose and flowing, hiding every contour.

My report contained none of this but put the case of how Celina could be of use as an asset and that I'd already formed a plan to leverage her in any way we saw fit.

My reports on Lenart were still thin. The children's non-existent.

I added Alarica to the list, making it clear she was sleeping with at least one member of her working family.

I didn't react when I got the usual response.

Instructions:

Observe. Report.

***

The day of the party started with Lenart already out of the house, the tyres on the gravel driveway waking me early. I pulled myself from under the duvet to look out of the window, only to lock eyes with a smile from Celina as she walked back to the house, a taxi heading into the distance at her back.

Dressing, I left my room, not wanting to be cornered in the small space and by my bed. By the time she'd risen the stairs I was heading in the opposite direction.

"Just the kids to send on their way, then it's our weekend," she said in an excited whisper.

I forced a smile, taking a deep breath as I passed her on the stairs, heading to the coffee machine.

She didn't join me for another hour; instead, she followed the children as they thumped down the stairs for the breakfast spread.

She made a big deal about the food I'd prepared, but the children barely acknowledged its existence.

Seeing the annoyance in Celina's expression, I volunteered to drop them both at their separate friend's houses, knowing each was the opposite side of the town; it would buy me at least an hour away from her attention.

Arriving back, I found the table spread with a feast; bread and cold meats, fruit and salad. Vapour fizzing from a bottle of champagne stood next to two tall, thin glasses. It was the most effort I'd seen her make for anything.

Still standing in the doorway to the dining room, Celina appeared through the door on the other side. She'd changed from her thick pyjamas into a thin pink negligee. I could see a hint of her body underneath, even with the silk dressing gown hanging either side.

Despite not staring, still I made out the darker skin around her nipples and the pink line where her legs met.

I took a deep breath as she looked up, feigning surprise as she put the tray of croissants on the table and wrapped the gown around her, with little effect.

"I didn't hear you come in," she said in a soft voice. I kept quiet, watching her smile at my silence. "Did the children get away okay?"

A gulp of air forced into my throat as I went to speak, my voice coming out a little hoarse.

"Yes, fine."

"I'm sorry they were so ungrateful this morning. I think

they were excited for their day."

"It's fine. I remember what it was like to be a teenager."

We both stood in silence. She looked at me with a smile in the corner of her mouth and I was looking anywhere but in her direction, whilst trying to concentrate on the table. "You shouldn't have done this, but thank you."

"You deserve it," she said. "Sit down and dig in." She pulled a chair out from around her side and I noticed she'd grouped all the food on the table, blocking all but two places where she'd set the mats next to each other.

"Let me freshen up," I said, using a phrase I'd never found the need for before.

I rushed up to my room and dropped off my coat, but rather than heading to the bathroom, I sat on the bed taking slow, deep breaths.

The party wasn't for another five hours. I had to think quick, but nothing came. I'd been gone too long already and with my breath settling, I headed back down the stairs.

In the end the meal wasn't the ordeal I thought it would be. She didn't jump me as I arrived at the table. We ate and talked like we had at the club, the alcohol settling my nerves.

She flirted, of course, on more than one occasion, letting the silk of her gown slip from her shoulder, showing the hint of her chest, but she didn't press herself against me and didn't force me to the floor or lunge toward me with pouting lips.

She was playing the long game; slow and subtle and I was afraid it might be working.

Before long, the first three hours had flown by. Checking my watch, I kicked myself for not being more alert, the second bottle of champagne having more than loosened my tension. I told Celina I had to prepare for the party, but she held me back, changing the conversation again and again.

It wasn't until there was an hour to go until the party that I realised why.

After collecting the dress from her room, excusing myself from getting dressed at her side, I found a long tear in the fabric which hadn't been there the few days before. I should have been angry and should have drawn a conclusion. Instead I smiled, heading to her bedroom to find her sat at her dresser, the silk dressing gown discarded to the bed. A wide smile on her face, her brows pinched together as I presented the long tear.

Without words she turned. I followed, my gaze falling to the bed and a beautiful but tiny black dress laid out beside the pink version Celina had chosen for herself in front of me only days before.

We didn't speak as I picked up the replacement and took it to my room, the alcohol showing me the funny side of how she'd engineered the situation; engineered me into an outfit that only just covered my ass and exaggerated my breasts.

Moments later, Celina stood at my door, a mirror image in all but the colour which had the same result on her. Her features raised in alarm and she pointed to my white bra straps pronounced either side of the dress's thin slivers of fabric, telling me in no uncertain terms that I had to lose it.

Bending to her will and thankful we had no more time to be alone, we soon finished the rest of the bottle and headed down the gravel driveway, along the short curb, past the cars lining the road and up to the house next door.

Soft piano welcomed us as Alarica opened the door, her polite smile widening as she saw our near-matching dresses. Her eyes locked with mine for a moment, our thoughts in sync for that second.

At her back, a stooped woman came through the thin crowd of guests dressed in suits, all with drinks in their hands. She welcomed us in, calling for Celina by name and shaking my hand as Alarica introduced me before Celina could get there.

Two observations leapt to my attention; Lenara's long, jet-black hair flowing to her shoulders, its lustre inconsistent with the deep lines creasing her face. The second were the burns and long-healed scars on her hands, the right of which much worse, pronounced with a stump where her pinkie should have been.

"You've met?" Celina said with surprise, seeming to be taking the words from Lenara's mouth.

"Earlier in the week. We found each other at the supermarket," Alarica said, her voice already building to a laugh. "She gave me such a fright when she followed me. I thought she was a private eye come to dig up my past."

"Well, nice to meet you," Lenara said in my direction, taking hold of Celina's hand and drawing her off. "Why don't you two get yourself something to drink while I show Celina to some people she won't have seen in an age."

With her words I turned and followed Alarica through the thin crowd of people, smiling at faces as they stared at the two of us, whilst wondering why they were looking so hard in my direction.

Alarica didn't speak until we were through the kitchen and into the laundry room, the shelves stacked high with catering boxes and crates of plates and glasses.

"She chose the outfit for you," she said, unable to hold back her giggles.

"How did you guess?" I replied.

"You look fucking hot, but like her younger, sexier sister."

"At least you didn't say her daughter," I replied, both of us bursting into laughter.

Once we settled, Alarica produced two tall glasses from the side and opened a small fridge, the light shining brightly on two stacked rows of champagne bottles.

With the cork out and expertly captured in her hand, she spoke in a low voice. "Where's the husband and the children?"

"He's out of the country and the kids are at friends."

"Convenient. What's she got planned?"

"I'm sure you can guess," I replied, burying my head in my free hand as I laughed.

"Are you going to?"

"No," I replied, cutting her off.

"Why not? Get it over with and she'll move on to someone else, I guess."

"I'm not like that."

"What, you wouldn't with a woman?" she said, tilting her head to the side, her thin eyebrows raised.

"Would you?" I shot back.

"I'm the one asking the questions. Would you?"

I shook my head. "It's where I work. I wouldn't sleep with either of them."

"Oh God, not the father," she replied, shaking her head. "What if she wasn't your boss?"

I didn't reply, the best I could do after the earlier bottles.

"Hah. You would," she said laughing.

"It depends how much I'd had to drink," I said, looking into my glass to her continued amusement.

"Another?" she said with a wide beam, holding up an empty glass.

"Very funny. We should mingle," I said and let her drag me back into the kitchen and out through the crowd as I tried to stop my topped-up bubbles from spilling.

We sat next to each other on golden-edged dining chairs in the corner of the long and wide room. With windows each end and crystal candelabra hung from the tall ceiling, the space seemed to have been designed exactly for this kind of event. The room bristled with conversation around three separate huddles.

"They know a lot of people," I said quietly, whilst looking around at the dark wooden furniture surrounding the room.

"Most of them are from his work," she said, her voice hushed. "They all live local too."

"Can't get away from the office. I know the feeling," I said, raising a smile. "This place looks like you've lived in it for years. From what we've seen for the past couple of weeks, I thought they'd stripped it bare?"

"It was, so I'm told. Not that I saw it beforehand. Lenara doesn't work and she's a tidy freak, but better at issuing orders that doing anything about it," she said, wiggling her fingers out in front as she spoke.

"Yeah? What's with the hands?" I said, looking down as she stopped.

"She's got some rare disorder. She can't feel things very well. Boiled her hands a few times and got her little finger trapped in a door."

"Ow," I replied.

"No, the opposite. That's the point," she said and burst out with laughter.

"You get along though?" I said, and she answered after a pause.

"I guess," she said with a big smile. "No, I'm kidding. It's fine. We get along fine." For the first time I saw a fake smile beaming in my direction. "I was kind of imposed on her though."

"By the husband," I said, turning to watch her expression.

"Yeah, of course. Who else?"

"Yeah, stupid thing to say," I replied, wondering what I could have meant.

I turned back to the party, watching a group of square-jawed men, all about mid-thirties, each filling out their wide suits with thick chests and arms. I'd seen plenty of these types of guys before.

"Does your boss run a nightclub?" I laughed and Alarica laughed back.

"They look like bouncers. Yes. Big sports fans, I think. Probably all played in college," she replied.

I turned to her, following her gaze back into the crowd and saw a tall guy who'd stopped all conversation as he walked in the room.

He was much older than most I'd seen so far at the party. Late forties, if not more senior. With jet-black hair on top of his head, the sides were white as a polar bear. A long

24

grey moustache ran across his top lip and he reminded me of a handsome version of J. Jonah Jameson, the boss of Spiderman's alter ego.

Like everyone in the room, I felt my mouth open. My breath paused as I waited for his next move.

"Who's that?" I said in a near whisper.

There was a few seconds pause before she gave a breathy reply. "That's Frank Bukia. My boss."

I felt a sudden wave of jealousy. It was him she was sleeping with him and it was plain to see why.

6

I turned to Alarica, her gaze still fixed in his direction as the conversation built back to its former volume.

"How long has it been?" I whispered as she continued to stare, only turning back at the realisation of what I'd said.

"Since what? What do you mean?" she replied, her cheeks flushing red.

"How long have you been sleeping with him?" I replied, reflecting a version of the smile she'd used when questioning me in the laundry room.

"No one can know. No, we haven't. No. Look, it was just once. Say nothing," she replied, leaning toward me with an urgency mirrored in her expression.

"I won't, don't be silly. We're friends now, right?"

"Friends," she said, her voice settling down as her look twisted around the room.

"So what's his day job then?" I said, watching her relax as I changed the subject. "Some big boss I'm guessing by the way they're treating him." Turning back, I watched everyone in the room continue to gravitate around Frank with a rolling chorus of laughter at his words.

"He's a big-deal doctor," she said, her gaze back in his direction.

"Was it recently?" I replied.

Alarica paused, the words hanging on her open lips. "Don't talk about it, please," she said, turning back to me. "At least not here."

I nodded and let our silence sit for a moment longer.

"I didn't think there was a hospital near?"

"He's not that sort of doctor. Well, he used to be. He works for a corporation. A specialist," she said, her face brightening as she continued to peer.

"You've got it bad. Like all these guys."

Her laugh was back. "Everyone's always fighting for his attention," she said, as if unable to take her eyes from him.

"I can see."

We sat silent for a moment longer, then as Alarica turned away we continued with idle chat, her shoulders relaxing as we each took turns to make observations pointed at each guest. A thick mono-brow that would better suit a dog. A badly fitting bra which made its owner's tits hang to the floor.

With other unkind comments, we sat in continual fits of laughter for a long while. Despite our enjoyment, Alarica couldn't help the occasional glance to Frank Bukia as he worked his way around the room.

I also kept an eye on Frank as he spoke with each guest at the party, even if just to give the shake of a hand or peck to a cheek.

I turned to Alarica as she halted in the middle of a cutting remark aimed at one of the wive's orange-peel upper arms.

Her gaze went to the centre of the room and following her dreamy stare, there he was with two long strides, rising over us. Alarica jumped to her feet.

I stood, his height looming like a statue. His shoulders seemed to span wider than Alarica and I standing together. The top of his head seemed darker this close, the white sides much whiter. He tipped a warm nod in Alarica's direction, turned and beamed his perfect whites in mine.

"Please introduce me to your friend," he said with more enthusiasm than I'd expected. Although his head turned towards Alarica, he fixed his gaze on me.

"This is… this is…" Alarica stuttered.

"Catarina," I added, turning to her. "Are you okay?"

"Fine, fine," she quickly said, waving away my concern.

"Pleased to meet you," Frank said. His slow, broad voice reverberated through my chest as I held my hand out. Our hands touched and we lingered, my gaze lost in his; his in mine.

We slid apart after what seemed like an age. "Frank," he said, with his smile still wide. His eyebrows lowered as if we'd shared some unspoken question neither of us had been able to answer.

"Likewise," I added, only just able to get the word out. I could feel Alarica's gaze boring into my side. "Alarica tells me you're a doctor?"

He glared a smile in Alarica's direction. "Does she now?"

"Some kind of specialist?" I added.

He turned to me and drew a broad grin. "An Orthopaedic Surgeon."

"You're not just an Orthopaedic Surgeon, are you?" Alarica said, her voice rising as she pushed her arm against mine.

Frank turned to her and tilted his head before turning to me with his cheeks bunching.

"Thanks, Al. My career is driven by an interest in the body's response to stimulation, or in my particular case, how we can reverse a lack of response in life-changing conditions."

"That sounds..." I said, then paused. "Interesting."

"More than interesting," Alarica replied before Frank could. "Some people can't feel any sensation. They can't feel touch, or even pain."

"Or pleasure," he added.

I took a drink from the flute to hide my hard swallow.

"Show Catarina the thing," Alarica said, turning between us, nearly jumping on the spot as she did.

Frank shook his head.

"What thing?" I said with a puzzled expression.

"It's just a cheap trick. Catarina won't want to know," he said, still shaking his head.

I kept quiet.

"Don't be silly," Alarica said, her voice childlike and high. "It's brilliant. Pleasssse."

Frank turned, looking over his shoulder. "You'll get me into trouble," he replied, returning with an apologetic smile.

"Go now," Alarica said, raising her eyebrows and leaning towards him. "She wants to know what this is all about. Don't you, Catarina?"

I didn't reply.

"Do you?" Frank said, and Alarica did a little dance.

"Of course she does," she replied on my behalf, grabbing my hand as I balanced the glass for a second time with the golden liquid rolling from side to side.

We arrived in the kitchen and she had me stand with my back to the work surface. We both watched the door as moments later Frank came through, his face a mixture of reluctance but resigned to corking Alarica's excitement.

She took Frank's champagne and jumped from one foot to the next.

He gave her a stern look and she calmed while she took my glass without asking.

"Don't look so worried," he said with a disarming smile. "It's nothing more than a subtle demonstration of what I investigate." As he spoke, he rubbed his hands together as if trying to warm them.

After a few seconds, his hands went towards my shoulder. "Are you sure you don't mind?"

With a nod being all I could manage, I watched his hands move, my eyes widening as I felt his warmth on my skin.

"Everyone knows when you pinch below the Trapezius, the muscle that runs from your neck to your shoulder, you can access a major group of nerves that run through your arms and chest. Certainly if you have a brother. Most people can excite pain. Do you mind?"

I nodded and felt a familiar withering feeling as my knees gave way a little, firming only as he released the pressure.

"But what people don't know is that with a light touch in the right place," he said, pausing, his fingers tracing the lines of my muscles, "you can excite a whole different feeling, if you just..." he paused again and I felt the pressure back in my shoulders and impulse of energy flashed up from between my legs. A wave of pleasure rippled up through my body, electricity crackled across my breasts.

"...Apply pressure in the right place."

Breath stole from my lungs and my eyes jammed shut. If Alarica hadn't been holding my arm I would have folded to the floor as the aftershocks of energy bucked my spine. I opened my eyes only as the pulse of pleasure subsided.

Still breathless, I could feel my nipples trying to break free from my dress.

"Oh my god," I said under my breath.

"Wow, that was the most intense reaction I've seen before," Frank said with a broad grin.

"Amazing, isn't it?" Alarica said.

I followed her gaze down to my dress and I pushed my arm across my chest to hide the two points tenting the thin material.

"Are you okay?" Frank asked. "I'm sorry if I embarrassed you."

"I'm fine, thank you," I said, still struggling to focus.

"I must get back or they'll miss me," he said, raising his eyebrows.

I stood quietly at Alarica's side and stared into her warm eyes. "Wow," I said, as we followed seconds behind him, back into the party still in full flow.

Sitting back at our seats and with Frank standing near, I was about to say something to Alarica when everyone in the room turned towards the door as a loud pleading voice came from the hall.

The voice soon built to anger and I watched three of the bigger men despatch themselves towards the sound without exchanging words.

I turned back just as Alarica stood to step in front of Frank.

7

"Sit down," Frank said, his voice firm and leaving Alarica in no doubt as she moved back around to her seat. "Just an uninvited guest," he added with a carefree laugh in his voice as he smiled toward me.

Although muffled, I caught some of the words from the corridor.

"You know there's no point," came a male voice before the door slammed, shutting out most of the volume from the voices rising outside.

"Can I get you ladies another drink?" Frank had turned back, but paused as one of the tall guests in a suit arrived at his shoulder, quickly leaning in as Frank accepted the message with a curt nod.

"Please excuse me," he soon said before heading through the door to the kitchen, followed by his messenger.

"That was something else," I said, looking at my chest to see if it was safe to move my arm, but Alarica still stared at the door which closed at Frank's back.

"Yeah," she replied half-heartedly, her lips only changing to a smile as she realised I stared in her direction. "Leave him alone," she said, her smile still fixed, before bursting into laughter.

"What was that all about?" I said as her laughter stalled.

"Beats me," she replied with a raise of her eyebrows. "Probably just someone upset they didn't get an invitation."

I gave a thin smile in reply.

"Give me your glass and I'll get us a refill." Almost snatching the glass from my hand, Alarica turned and headed after Frank.

Turning away as the door swung closed at her back, I studied the room. The three large guys had re-joined the party, their suits straight, but red-faced and puffed with effort as they took their glasses from their plus ones and slipped back into conversation.

As I regained my composure from Frank's display, my

gaze bounced from face to face. With a habit I had even before training, each set of features collated and catalogued, ready to retrieve in an instant should they be seen out of context. All this went on without my effort, but the process stopped dead as I spotted Celina stood at Lenara's side, both of them gazing at me. They giggled and headed in my direction.

Blowing out a deep breath as they approached, I chanced a glance to the kitchen door in hope Alarica would be charging to my aid. But no.

I stood as they arrived, knowing I had too much cleavage on show already without them looking down from above.

"You have a lovely house, Mrs Bukia," I said, holding my attention on her.

"Lenara, please, and thank you. They've done a good job. I'm sure we'll settle back in soon."

"It's already exquisite," I added.

She bunched a smile back at me. "Celina has been telling me all about how well you're getting along. It's so nice when these things come together," she replied, glancing back to Celina who wore a wide grin.

"Yes. She's so good to me and does so much around the house. Too much, I keep telling her. She needs to kick back a bit and enjoy herself," Celina said with her gaze fixed on mine as I turned with a forced smile.

"And so beautiful," Lenara said.

To my alarm, I watched as she looked me up and down.

"You're turning all the heads. I don't think I'll invite you next time. I'm supposed to be the centre of attention." The pair burst into laughter as I tried to work out if it was meant as a compliment. "Of course I'm joking. You're welcome around here anytime, except when Celina needs you. You look a little flushed, my dear?"

"I'm fine, thank you," I replied, but I could feel my cheeks blazing.

"I hope Frank hasn't been showing you his blasted

party trick," she said, laughing more towards Celina than me.

With that they drifted off together, Celina glancing back over her shoulder and winking as her behind swayed, kicking up the loose back of the short dress. I hoped people couldn't see as much of my ass as I could of hers.

"Don't worry," Alarica said before I realised she was back at my side. "We'll sort her out tonight. Take this."

Her hands were full of four flutes topped off with light, golden bubbles. I took the two glasses she gestured in my direction and watched as she scurried after the plotting pair, handing off the glasses and taking their empties.

Alarica tilted her head in my direction, gesturing for me to follow into the kitchen where we found Frank and one of his thickly-built dinner guests. Their conversation stopped as we arrived.

"Nate, this is Catarina," Frank said.

I shook the large offered hand, nodding a shy greeting.

Frank turned and nodded in my companion's direction with a warm smile before turning back to me. "Catarina is Mr and Mrs Rozman's au pair."

"Nice to meet you," Nate replied in a deep voice.

"Nice to meet you, too," I said. "Do you work with Mr Bukia?"

"Frank, please," Frank said, answering the question himself. "Nate is one of my best guys. He's been with me for... must be ten years now."

"Praise indeed," I said, trying my best to tear my attention away from Frank's eyes.

"I've got to make a call, but Nate, why don't you introduce Catarina to the rest of our people?" Frank said, his stare holding in my direction.

"No problem," Nate answered, and he offered his hand out toward the other kitchen door.

The next couple of hours comprised dull conversation with Nate by our side for the first hour, along with Alarica, except when she'd disappear to freshen the glasses.

I held myself back from drinking too much, but I soon

felt the effects hampering my ability to take in all the information for my report tomorrow.

After excusing myself to use the bathroom and then coming out of the first-floor washroom, Alarica greeted me, heading up the stairs with a wide grin as I appeared.

"I think they're both cooked," she said, trying not to let herself dissolve into a fit of laughter. At her back I saw Celina stumbling through the opening with her arm around Lenara in a similar state.

"I'll take her home. It looks like she'll sleep well tonight," I replied with my eyebrows raised.

"You can thank me later," Alarica replied.

I was about to turn to ask the obvious question when, as we came level on the stairs, Celina tripped, only just able to stay upright.

Rushing down the stairs, I took her arm over my shoulder and I walked her to the front door, politely refusing help from Nate. Turning back, I watched Lenara being helped up the stairs by Alarica. It looked like we'd both have freedom to do what we wanted tonight.

Moments later, I'd manhandled Celina up the stairs, stripping off her clothes with ease. Like me, she only wore three items.

Once naked she seemed to have a moment of clarity. My heart jumped at the thought I'd been played, but after a few tearful attempts to get me to jump in beside her, she turned, snoring within seconds.

Leaving the room, my gaze fell on the clock. It was only nine in the evening. Alarica had put something in their drinks, I was sure. I'd seen the sudden symptoms before. I knew what to look for and I couldn't help but feel grateful for letting me off what could have been an awkward night. At least I knew it was one of her motivations.

Locking the house, I turned the lights off and wrapped up in my towelling dressing gown. I climbed to the top of the three-storey house and stood at the tall hallway window, watching the neighbours with my clear view from high over the fence.

With the house still brightly lit, I saw shapes, people moving around inside. I caught glances of Alarica, hints of Frank amongst the others. Occasionally, the party moved outdoors, small congregations smoking as they talked and always with a glass to hand.

I soon felt the effects of the alcohol bearing down and I found myself staring into the darkness of the trees at the bottom of the garden.

Turning away from the window, I took a deep breath. It was still early and I had the house to myself, but I'd already searched everywhere I could think of.

Despite trying to think of anything else useful I could do, I instead sent a short report describing the night with Frank and Alarica.

The reply was almost instant.

Instructions:

Observe Fifty-Six. Report.

8

I woke early the next morning; much earlier than Celina. Peering through her open door, I watched the covers for the gentle rise and fall before I got on with the chores; my diligence programmed since my arrival.

It was almost midday before I heard the first stirrings upstairs and with a coffee in hand I approached with soft steps. She watched me through the door, squinting from behind the edge of the white duvet with her head jammed against the headboard like she'd given up on a full rise.

"Are you okay?" I said, lowering the cup to her bedside table as I perched on the edge of the bed.

"I think so," she said, seeming more than a little unsure. "My head feels strange," she added, her voice dry and croaky. "What happened last night?"

"I think you may have gotten a little carried away," I replied, trying not to sound like a mother. I watched her consider my words, her stare going through me as if she rummaged through fragments of memory.

"I remember having a good time." She tried a smile, but couldn't get it to stick. "We can get a little excitable," she said, her words slow. "When we're together."

"Lenara was in the same state as you."

"A state?" she said, her eyes widening for a moment, only to shrink as the light forced its way in.

"It wasn't too bad. You didn't make a scene."

"What time did we get back?"

"About nine."

"Wow. I needed to slow down on the bubbles. Then what happened?"

"I put you to bed."

"And?" she asked, still squinting.

"I got you undressed."

"And?"

"Then I went to bed. In my room."

"So I didn't...?" she paused midway.

"You didn't do anything," I replied.

"I didn't miss anything," she said, correcting me.

I couldn't help but laugh. She wasn't worried about what she'd done, or we'd done. She was just concerned she'd lost the memory.

"I'm not sure what you mean, but no, you didn't miss anything."

"Good, but you got me undressed?"

"Yes."

"Did you like what you saw?"

I laughed and stood, telling her I'd see her later.

"What time are the children back?" I said as I went through the door.

"Midday," she said. "Tomorrow." The words were quiet, but I still heard.

I took a deep breath.

"I'm going next door to see if I can help them clean up from last night," I shouted from the top of the stairs.

9

From the street the house looked as if the party had never happened. It was the afternoon, but still I expected cars of the stragglers from the night before to be hanging around.

Knocking at the door, Alarica greeted me, beaming with delight.

"I thought I'd come and give you a hand to clean up."

"Come in, but no need. The caterers took care of everything," she replied, leading me through to the kitchen.

From what I could see, the house was spick and span with the furniture pulled back into place. I couldn't see a single sign there had been a party.

"How was it after I left?" I said as she pulled two cups from a cupboard and prepared coffee.

"I was going to ask you the same."

I shook my head and laughed. "I put her to bed and had the rest of the night to myself," I replied. "You saved me from a difficult night. Thank you."

"I really don't know what you could mean," she replied, stifling laughter as she poured water from the kettle. "You should have come back over."

"I didn't want to cramp your style."

Her eyes widened as her finger shot to her mouth and she shook her head. I kept quiet as she added the milk and quickly led me outside to a bench at the bottom of the garden, a good walk from the house.

"Sorry," I said as we both sat crossed-legged on the wooden seat.

"It's fine, just don't say anything like that around the house."

"Okay. So what did you get up to then?"

"Nothing. We put Lenara to bed when you left and the last of the guests seemed to drift off about midnight."

"And?"

"I invited him into the woods for a walk," she said, holding her hands open in the air. "But he thought better of it."

"You've done it in the woods?" I said, my eyes wide.

"No," she said. "Not yet anyway. We were away last time."

"Oh, do tell," I said, surprising myself at being more than a little intrigued to hear the details.

"What's to tell?"

I raised my eyebrows and grinned back at her. She shrugged then leant in close as she spoke with a lowered voice.

"We were all on holiday. Lenara took the children off to some theme park. I had a headache and Frank hung around to do some urgent work. We drank wine, which did wonders for my pain and he finished his emails within minutes, so we enjoyed the drink on the sofa."

"How did it happen? Did you know it was going to?"

"No, I didn't. It snuck up on me. One minute he was pouring the second glass, the next we were finishing the third bottle and we kissed."

"And then?"

"And then, you know."

"You had sex?"

"We made love, right there on the living room floor."

"What was it like?" I cringed as I heard my eager voice, but couldn't stop myself.

"It was amazing. It lasted what seemed like hours. He was all over me. Covering me in kisses, everywhere."

"What did it feel like?" I said.

She paused and I realised my mistake.

"Well, you know, it felt like it feels." She paused again, looking me in the eye. "You know, don't you?"

I didn't reply, other than with a raise of my eyebrows.

"No way. You've never had sex? What are you… Twenty?"

"Twenty-one."

"Still, come on. You're kidding me, right?"

"No."

"Oh my god," she blurted out, her free hand jumping

to mine. "Wow. Oh my god, I'm really sorry. I wouldn't have got Frank to do that thing if I'd have known. Oh god."

"Don't worry, it was great. I mean it was fine," I said, trying to roll back the words.

"So you've never had sex?"

"No," I said, shaking my head. In the back of my mind I could hear myself screaming. Why was I saying these things? Why was I being so open with someone I'd really only known for a few days?

"Wait. Are you a lesbian? I mean a proper one."

"No," I replied, pausing. "I don't think so," I added, alarming the voice inside my head.

"So you've never had sex with a man or a woman?" she said slowly.

I drew a deep breath. "No."

"Are you one of those asexuals? Poor you, you're missing so much."

"What's an asexual?"

"Someone who isn't interested in sex. Someone who doesn't get turned on."

"Oh god no, almost the opposite. I find most people attractive. Men, women, it doesn't seem to matter," I said, pushing my concern further away.

"But you've never…"

"No."

"Why the hell not? You're gorgeous. You must get queues down the road trying to get into your pants. Wait, sorry, is there something wrong with your muschi?"

"My what?" I said, looking back with raised eyebrows.

"Your downstairs. You know. What do you call it?" she said, pointing down between my legs.

"I don't call it anything," I replied, my brow scrunched.

"You must call it something. Was it disfigured in some horrible accident? Let me see," she said, leaning forward, peering at the crotch of my jeans.

"No, there's nothing wrong with me down there. At least I don't think so," I said, straightening my legs.

40

"How do you know?"

"It looks all right."

"Compared to what?"

"Pictures I've seen."

"You mean porn?"

"I guess so."

"So you do know what it's called then," she said with a knowing smile in my direction. "Just call it a pussy and be done with it. It sounds better in German though."

I raised an eyebrow.

"What? It's a lovely way to describe it. It makes me think of a warm blanket of fur and it purrs when you stroke it." She burst out laughing.

I struggled to keep a straight face until suddenly her expression dropped and she spoke slowly.

"Maybe you can't have an orgasm?"

"Oh, I can," I said, trying to stifle a wide grin. "I think I nearly had one in your kitchen last night."

She laughed and took a deep breath, holding it as she stared back in awe.

"I'm so confused. Do you want to?"

"Want to what?"

"Come on, do you want to pop your cherry?"

"I guess so, eventually."

"Man or woman?"

"I don't know."

"It doesn't matter, but they're so much different."

"You like women too?" I asked without meaning to.

"I prefer men, but I've dabbled."

It was my turn to laugh, but as I slowed my breathing I saw Lenara walking towards us wrapped in a silk robe, squinting, her face hanging a mirror image of Celina's expression.

Alarica lowered her voice, leaning in as she saw her employer cross the grass towards us. "Mission accepted."

After thanking me for offering to help with the clear up, the conversation with Lenara was much the same as the first part of the conversation with Celina. She was pleased to hear that Celina was in the same state last night and this morning and promised to speak with the champagne supplier for the poor quality of one or more of the bottles they'd shared.

I soon left with a promise to pass across an invitation to Celina for lunch tomorrow, which I did when she woke. The hangover kept her laid low for the rest of the day and our paths didn't cross until after her lunch with Lenara the next day.

With the food shopping and collecting the children, I didn't see Celina until the afternoon. She met me outside as I hung washing on the long line.

"I'm sorry I didn't see you much yesterday. That bad bottle of champagne ruined my plans."

"It's fine. I was very busy with the chores anyway."

"You do too much," she said, stepping with me as I moved along the line. "That said, I hope you don't mind but I've offered your services next week. I'm not sure I told you, but the kids and I are going with Lenart to a thing next week. We'll be away for six days. It'll be such a bore but I've got to show willing.

"I would have invited you along, but you'd hate it and Lenart wants some time with just the family, not that he ever sees you. So I don't know what the problem is. Anyway, talking over lunch with Lenara, she's too much fun, she mentioned that Alarica is going home for a week and Frank is off on business, too. So I offered your services to help with the house. I hope you don't mind. She doesn't get on too well on her own. They'll pay you what Alarica gets and of course we'll still be paying you."

"It's fine," I said. I already knew about the trip and about Alarica going home, too. My kindness to Lenara and the offer of help with the clearing up were not mere gestures.

10

The day came around quickly.

The previous morning I'd said goodbye to Alarica as she renewed her promise to get on with her project as soon as she returned. With the Rozman's packed off, I headed around to fifty-six to find the house all but empty. The children had already left for school and Frank had gone away early that morning.

With the house looking pristine, I found Lenara making coffee in the kitchen.

I took a deep breath at the silence, hoping I wasn't in for a rerun of the last few weeks I'd had with Celina. Lenara was quick to offer Alarica's room if I didn't fancy the very short walk home to an empty house each night.

As I politely declined, she sat me down with a coffee and told me to relax. She wanted a chat.

It turned out to be more of an interview. Although smiling throughout and making pleasant noises, the questions drilled in quick succession. Where was I from? How had my home life been? Siblings? School?

I knew the information off by heart, being well drilled in all the details, but still I was forced to elaborate to fill in some gaps I didn't realise existed.

"So what do your parents do?" she said. "Sorry for all the questions, but I'm such a nosey old bat. It's either that or the washing up," she said, laughing.

"They're both retired now," I said. "My dad was in the military."

"Which branch?"

"RAF. An engineer," I replied without pause.

"And your mother?"

"A nurse, then a housewife."

"And what made you leave and come here to clean up other people's mess and look after their kids?"

"Life experience," I replied. "My family has very little money, so I have to work while I see the world."

"Are you planning to stick around?"

"For the next six months, I guess. I'm under contract."

She smiled back at those words. "And you seem to get on with Celina?"

"Yes," I said. "She's very nice, as is the rest of the family."

She made a contented purr. "Well, she likes you too. She hardly speaks of anything else these days," she said, raising her eyebrow. "I exaggerate, of course."

I nodded and she asked what I thought of Alarica.

"We seem to have hit it off."

"Yes, she has taken quite a shine to you. It won't do her any harm to have some friends of her own age."

"Sorry to ask, but have I done something wrong?" I said, still more than a little surprised about the questioning.

Lenara sat back in her seat and puffed out air, her hands out square on her knees. "No. It's me that should be sorry. I was just a little surprised with the way they talked about you. I've seen it before. A woman comes in and puts up a front, tricking people."

"That's not me. What you see is what you get."

"Yes, I can see that. You seem like a sweet girl," she said, but her eyes still narrowed as if she didn't trust her own words.

"Can I ask, maybe I'm a little naïve, but what is it these women are trying to get?"

Lenara laughed. "Sorry, it's rude for me to laugh, but you're so delightful. It's the men, my dear. They're after the men. They buddy up with the wives and their friends. They make it seem that the beautiful girl with the bright blue eyes and perfect white teeth is not a threat to their lives, to their relationship. Then they strike."

"Sorry, what do you mean 'they strike'?"

"They ensnare the husband. Flashing their pert breasts and perfect tight asses and if the man isn't protected and you're not vigilant, they've got him. Men are so weak. They think with their genitals and once it's happened, it's hard work to get them back." She sobbed, pulling a tissue from the box under the table by the side of the chair.

"Has it happened to you?" I replied in a quiet voice. I watched her head tilt back and forward. "Was it Mr Bukia?"

She shot a look back for a moment, then her eyes seemed to brighten again. "No. He's a good man and I protect him. He's my second husband. My first was weak. A sucker for big tits and a smile. Sorry for my vulgarity but because of my condition I find it hard to get pleasure from relations. I have to be extra vigilant to protect my interests. Do you know what I mean?"

"Yes, and I understand," I replied, not too sure if I did.

"But you're sweet. Just remember, someday you'll be a wife, I hope, and you need to be on your guard."

"I'll watch out."

With that the conversation ended as she lost all interest in asking me questions, instead heading up the stairs to fix her makeup whilst I was to make myself at home. She told me to do whatever I felt was necessary; she was going out and would be back with the children after they'd eaten dinner out.

Within minutes she'd left and I'd searched out the brightly-coloured upright vacuum cleaner and hung a duster from my back pocket. Circling around the house on my journey up the two flights of stairs, I'd soon confirmed the house to be as pristine as it had first looked.

Still, on the top floor I plugged in the vacuum and began to push it over the thick piled carpet, keeping my head pointed down at the floor with my gaze roving the rooms.

The first, a girl's room; the teenage daughter I'd yet to meet. The room ordered but with a wooden packing crate in the corner, it was the first hint they'd only just moved back in.

The second, a small bathroom; a toilet and shower sandwiched beside a boy's room. He was younger than his sister with small, brightly-coloured plastic bricks strewn across the floor.

The third, a spare room with a double bed filling the space between the walls, the light brown duvet spread evenly across its surface, the edges pulled tight and tucked neat to the mattress. The wardrobe full of blankets and bedding.

Taking the time to run the nozzle over each of the stairs, I carried the noisy machine down to the next level and scoured the hall where I got the first hint of new paint still in the air.

I could already tell the house was much bigger than the one I'd come from, its design completely different; its external dimensions deceptive.

The next room was the most disordered so far, even compared with the young boy's. Make up bottles and tubes lay spilt from a small bag on a dresser, their names and uses alien to me; the depth of my experience taken from deep greens and blacks of camo paint, not this subtle rainbow of shades. Clothes were strewn across the floor, the wardrobe door wide open. A suitcase lay on the base of the wooden furniture. The double bed in the centre ruffled. The covers to the side as if the occupant had woken late, packing in a panic, straighteners and a hairdryer put to use, then discarded on a chair to cool.

It was Alarica's room.

I pulled the door closed and headed to the next, finding a cupboard; a hot water tank and towels hiding inside.

Next was the master bathroom with a corner bath and a shower, too. In the opposite corner, the bright white of the tiles and enamel sparkled as the morning sun streamed through the wide frosted windows.

The marital bedroom came after and a hairless pale mannequin's head greeted me, staring back from the dressing table. I took a step in and saw other than the bed was larger, it was much like the spare room with crisp clean folds and tucks, the beside tables clear of any clutter and an alarm clock on one side, a box of paper tissues on the opposite and a tall thin lamp sat on each.

A dark wooden wardrobe, teak or mahogany, lined the far wall, offsetting the white patterned wallpaper wrapping the room in brightness, broken only by a second room; a small ensuite bathroom. A toilet and a sink were the only furniture.

The next room stood apart from the rest. A study with a wide desk in the centre and a chair the other side with its back to a tall window. Any occupier would have a full view of the door and that of a computer screen offset to its left.

A keyboard and a pen rested on top of a green blotter running most of the width of the desk.

Pushing the vacuum cleaner over the threshold, I saw tall bookcases obscuring both walls to the right. The shelves were crammed but ordered, with tall, thick medical books one side and short, fat fiction lined up on the other.

To my left, the built-in wardrobe seemed to be a hangover from its previous occupation as a bedroom and my gaze lingered on the intricate inlaid details. I could smell the sweetness of new wood, its intensity growing as I pushed the appliance closer.

Wrapping up in the room, I pushed the head of the noisy beast around the edges of the hall and along the length of the skirting board until I reached the master bedroom door. I turned off the noise at the head of the machine and strolled to the bedside, plucking a tissue from the box.

Blowing my nose in gesture only, I took the chance to stare at the wall to the right of the door and I saw what I'd been looking for, despite there being nothing obvious; the wall stopped too soon. Or the wardrobe on the other side started early.

It was either very deep, walk-in perhaps, or hid another room inside.

I glided the head of the vacuum across the rest of the surfaces, my gaze scouring for more inconsistencies in the walls of the ground floor. When I finished, I made a coffee, concentrating only on replaying the image in my mind of what I'd seen, not able to break a rule of my craft we needed to keep to in the twenty-first century.

11

During the rest of the week I settled into a rhythm; spending half of each day at fifty-six doing chores and cooking dinner, all with one eye searching for flaws in the architecture whilst avoiding the study other than was necessary.

I was sure the wardrobe would be locked, although I didn't test the old-fashioned keyhole standing indented in the centre.

While back in the Rozman's, I sent long reports of my observations, but getting nothing of interest back.

Instructions:

Observe. Report.

I wondered what would happen if I missed a report. I wondered perhaps if there was something wrong with the keyboard the other end.

The Rozman's and the rest of the Bukia's were back within twenty-four-hours of each other, signalling the end of a dull six days. Frank arrived with a puppy and I could all but imagine the children's explosive reactions.

The Rozman's brought back stressed expressions, as if they needed to settle back into their personal space and climb into their individual orbits which rarely collided. The children were indifferent as I greeted them at the door. Lenart gave a smile, peering past me to check everything had survived their absence. Celina carried a sly grin, licking her lips as she passed in to the hall.

They each sat at the dining room table and ate the lunch I'd prepared for their arrival whilst I aimed my excitement at the new member of the Bukia family, watching the flash of interest in both the children.

The boy's eyes lit as he turned to his father, only to be dashed by a firm glare in response, a short negative coming soon after.

"Why did you do that?" he said, finding me in the

kitchen a few moments later.

Turning from the counter, I saw the door closed at his back.

"Sorry?" I replied with a question in my tone.

"Why did you put me in that position?" he said, his thick eyebrows bunching.

"Um," I replied, forcing a wide look of surprise. "I didn't mean to put anyone in any position."

"Well you did. I had to let him down. I had to be the bad guy."

"I'm really sorry. That wasn't my intention," I said, stepping back as he edged towards me.

"Okay," he said, stopping. "Please don't do that again."

"I won't," I replied, adding another apology as he turned.

That was my first interaction with Lenart alone and my first insight into his character. I had to hold my anger, stopping myself from lashing out and smashing a plate across the top of his head before he pulled open the door.

With a deep breath I continued to clear the table, Lenart smiling in my direction when our glances crossed, a picture of reason to all around. Maybe now I knew why Celina held her attention to everyone else.

With the place straight after the big lunch, the family scattered to their separate corners of the house; the children each to their rooms, Celina to the garden to help Brad with clearing weeds and Lenart to the living room, his feet up on a stool and a short glass of brown liquor at his side.

I'd finished for the day and when a knock at the door interrupted my thoughts, I hurried away to accompany Alarica as the new puppy dragged her down the track between houses, racing to explore the woods.

"Thanks for helping while I was away," she said as we left earshot of the two houses. The light had already started to dull through the canopy as the path headed deeper into the thick trees.

"I didn't do much. Just ran the vacuum around a few

times."

"You kept her company and stopped her thinking too much."

"In all honesty I hardly saw her," I replied, trying not to laugh as she struggled to control the black Alsatian who at twelve weeks old was already strong enough to lead the excursion. "We had a chat on the first morning."

"Oh, I'm really sorry. Did she interrogate you?"

"Interrogate? Ha," I said, then stifled my laughter. "She came on a bit strong, but I think I won her round."

"You did. Believe me, you did."

"She was talking like I was plotting to steal her husband."

"I know. She went through some bad stuff with her first and you know how everyone gravitates around Frank," she said, looking away into the distance. "She has to put up with that, too."

"I understand. It was fine. She offered me your room, not the spare, rather than take the thirty-second walk to my bed. That reminds me, for someone who cleans and tidies other people's mess, you don't seem to take the habit to heart."

"You mean my room?" she replied, only glancing back in my direction.

"Yeah, it was a tip."

"That wasn't me," she replied. "Lenara does that every time I go away. You had the chat and you won her over. I had the chat and didn't quite convince and now she thinks I'm sleeping with Frank."

I stayed silent. I was lost for the words which would comfort her, but then I let my thoughts slip.

"You have though," I said quietly, but still she heard.

"I know, but she can't know. I think she thought we were away together because our trips coincided."

"That's unfair. You've got to see your family," I replied, the words tailing off as she turned to face me with a sly grin.

"I didn't make it home," she said, her face beaming.

"So you did go away with him?" I replied, leaving my mouth wide.

"Oh my god, it was amazing. I stayed in the hotel the whole week while he was coming and going to business meetings. I'm surprised I can walk now. Every time he'd come back we'd be at it like rabbits. I'm exhausted."

"Holy shit," was all I could reply and then lost my words again as I watched her strain to keep control of the dog, her face stretched in a wide smile. "So she was right to be paranoid about him."

Her smile dropped a little. "I guess so, but she couldn't know. Anyway, she doesn't treat him well. She can't..." she stopped herself and paused. "A man like Frank has needs that she can't satisfy."

"She told me she had some issues."

"Yeah. She had an accident a long time ago, got brain damage. It must have been when her son was just a baby. She lost complete sensation of her body. It got better though, but she still has issues feeling pain and can't feel when it's in," she said, raising her eyebrows. "And can't reach a climax."

"And he told you this?" I said, raising my brows.

"Yes. He's not a bad man."

"I didn't say he was," I replied, putting my hand on her shoulder.

"We all need pleasure in our lives and it just so happens we're the perfect match. I know he loves his wife and I'm fine with that, but she's more like his sister than anything else. It's been so long."

"Do you think he loves you?"

She grinned. "Yes, but not like a sister," she replied, her eyes seeming to mist over.

"Do you love him?"

"I do," she said without pause, her arm circling into mine and she hugged at my shoulder.

"And are you enough for him?" I said. "A man like that must be hard to please."

She laughed again. "He seemed pretty satisfied to me.

Well, at least for a couple of hours after." She burst into laughter.

I didn't, not sure how I felt.

"You think I'm a bad person, don't you?" she added, her smile gone.

"No," I replied with only a slight pause.

"Then I'd better not tell you what he wants to do next," she replied, her wide grin having returned.

"What?"

"Maybe I was a little untruthful when I said I could satisfy him, on my own at least," she burst in to giggles, but I kept my face straight, my brow remaining furrowed.

I had no idea what she meant.

"Anyway, that's enough about me. Oh, and please don't breathe a word of this to anyone. No matter what you think."

"Of course not," I replied, knowing it was a lie; knowing I'd pass on the key bit of intelligence as soon as I could.

We walked for a good hour, not revisiting the details of her trip again. We headed deeper into the woods which seemed to be never ending, only turning back when we realised how far we'd gone and the dog hadn't shown even the first signs of tiring.

Following the long path back, we split with a peck on each cheek as the hard-packed mud turned to gravel between the houses.

"Same time tomorrow?" Alarica said.

"Sure," I replied, "but this time can I ask Celina if the kids can come along?"

She looked at me with her eyebrow raised. I looked back with a slight smile and she knew I was planning something.

"Okay," she replied and turned with a kiss blown in my direction.

Arriving back at the house, I watched Lenart snoring in his chair. Someone had switched the TV off and beside him a tall bottle sat half drained of its brown contents. Whoever had turned off the TV must have removed the glass from his hand as he slept, his fingers still circled around the missing round shape.

With the rest of the house silent, I found Celina in the garden with her feet curled under her and gaze fixed on a trashy paperback in her hand. Still she spotted me as I stood in the open doorway and beckoned me out, waving with the book still in her hand.

She continued to read as I crossed the short grass and I spotted the empty bottle at the foot of the bench. It nestled next to two glasses. One empty, the other at the half mark.

"Did you get lost?" she said, folding the corner of the page.

"No, but that beast of a dog takes some walking. I'd never seen those woods before. It would be so easy to get lost."

"They look scary to me," she replied, looking for her glass.

"Oh, but I love it," I replied. "You only have to walk for a few minutes and you feel like you're in another world. It's so secluded, so private. You could get up to anything out there."

Celina's head snapped up, her eyes pinching as a smile grew on her face.

"We should get a dog," she replied, knocking back the last of the wine.

12

The very next afternoon Celina, the children and I set off with Alarica, soon joined by Lenara hobbling down the path when she saw the size of the expedition.

She linked arms with Celina, marvelling at the view as the children took it in turns to take control of the dog, handing back when his power proved too much.

By the end of the hour-long excursion, I'd fired up the children with the intended energy and motivation, knowing they had to join forces with their step mum and apply full bargaining power and emotional blackmail to their father.

Still, he blamed me.

Later that evening he'd somehow raised himself from his whiskey-fuelled slumber after the heavy meal; a meal at which I'd avoided his eye contact as the children and Celina drove up the pressure. With dessert, a steamed mess of cake and custard, he ended with a great smile and proclaimed they would go next weekend and visit some pups.

I found out soon after it had all been for show. With tangy breath I smelt before I saw him, he cornered me in the utility room as I sorted washing. I hadn't seen the children since dinner, Celina a short while ago, likely in bed watching TV or dozing off the two bottles from dinner she hadn't been allowed to share; Lenart had already made it clear. The hired help doesn't drink at dinner.

If only he knew the strength and training I held in my wrists. What I lacked in bulk I gained from coaching by the very best. He didn't know this as he stepped closer, all the while telling me I had to be a good girl and do as he said or there would be consequences.

He wouldn't let me bend his family to my will.

Instead of lashing out, locking his head under my arm and smashing it with a single blow against the counter, I hung my face with fear, eyes widening, breath drawing in short bursts.

Still, he came forward and watched, his mouth curling

as my eyes dropped to the obvious bulge at his crotch, my thoughts faltering just for a second.

Not you, too, for goodness's sake.

"Do you enjoy being told off?" he said.

I shook my head.

"I bet you're wetter than an otter's pocket," he slurred, jumping forward, his arms lunging in a pincer.

I let a gasp slip and dived under his arms, his senses too dulled to react.

Jumping through the doorway, I cast a glance at my back to see he'd barely reacted, turning only as I let the door slam. That was the point I decided he had to be dealt with.

Wedging my bedroom door against a night time revisit, I made my plans.

It was easy to avoid him in the morning; with the working week ahead he'd be back into his routine of early mornings and late nights passed out in front of the TV.

But I couldn't rely on that alone. I couldn't rely on evasion and there was no way I could let him think he could touch me.

I'd break it off and stuff it down his throat before I'd let that thing anywhere near me.

No. My approach would be more subtle and give me control.

In normal circumstances I'd set up a drop off for what I wanted, but I'd already been told I was on my own.

I didn't need any supplies to Observe and Report. Instead, I had to make my own contacts who could get what I needed and in a large enough quantity.

On the morning trip with Alarica to the supermarket, I spoke with her about an occasional bout of sleeplessness and she was quick to offer a solution. Knocking on the door only five minutes after our trip, she handed me a small clear plastic bag of five pills.

Xanax, she explained, and I listened with intent as she told me the dose for a good night's sleep with a warning to avoid alcohol or I'd wake with a devil of a hangover.

"Sounds familiar," I said, laughing. She joined in.

Within the hour I'd crushed two down to a powder and poured them in the half-full bottle of brown liquor from the cabinet in the lounge, the tablets soon dispersing. Two glasses should be all he would have of an evening and would keep him out of trouble, but I'd need a bigger supply if this was my longer-term solution.

A few days later and on what had now become our regular lone dog walk each afternoon, I questioned Alarica on how she'd got the tablets, telling her how well they'd worked.

After warning of their addictive nature and that I should only have two or three a week, she explained they were prescription only, unless you knew a friend.

"You make friends quickly," I said. "You've only been in town for two months."

"Okay. Maybe not friends, but I know where to get this stuff from. I can get you anything you want."

"Like?" I replied, trying my best to maintain my innocence.

"What? Don't tell me you're a virgin at that, too? Did your parents lock you away while you grew up?"

"I've never tried drugs, if that's what you mean. Do you use drugs?" I said, giving a worried puppy-dog frown.

"Hey, don't worry, I'm not an addict. It's just sometimes nice to add a little extra into the mix, or maybe you might need something and don't want to go to the local quack."

"Like sleeping pills. I get it."

"Or something to help keep it up all the way into the night," she replied, smirking. "Look, I'll get more for you tomorrow."

"Shall I come with you?"

"No. I say they're my friends, but they're not. They'll eat you alive and not in a good way," she replied.

I gave her a blank look.

"Oh yeah, I guess you've never done that either."

I continued with my blank reply and she changed the

subject.

By the morning we'd agreed that I would come along, but only into the town where they'd do the deal. I'd wait in the shops whilst she went off.

We took the Bukia's car and drove the half hour to the next town over, parking beside a strip mall of fifteen single-storey shops in what I could tell was not the nicest part of town. We went our separate ways on leaving the car; I headed to a convenience store and she walked along the mall front.

In the store I took off my short bomber jacket, turning it inside out, switching from the bright red to a dark navy blue, its design showing no difference. I pulled a baseball cap from my pocket and wound my hair in a tight pony, stuffing it under the hat after pushing on thick-rimmed sunglasses.

I was back out along the strip quick enough to see her disappear around the edge of the front and I followed her quick pace. Catching sight as I turned the corner, I watched as she headed down a long street, her head swishing side to side. She was observing, most likely looking for the police and not one of her friends following.

Her observations continued as she walked, turning this way and that down streets and alleys, making me close up to within five car lengths to stop from losing her. Still, I lost sight as she turned another corner. She'd headed right down a long line of houses, the streets lined with trash overflowing from their round metal cans. Broken glass littered the road; glass from the streetlights, I realised as I looked upward.

The street looked as if the town authorities were told to avoid the area unless they had police along for the ride. I took these observations in just a second. She was the only thing missing from the picture and I had to walk on.

I couldn't stand in the street glancing around or someone would soon notice me as being out of place.

It was then I heard a door slam at my back and I crossed the road, using the opportunity to catch Alarica in my peripheral vision to my left.

Taking a second glance at the door she'd just come

from, it was one of many which had glass missing, but the only one where both panels were filled with low grade, flaked wooden board.

I had my back to her and I was heading in the wrong direction. She'd expect to meet me back at the mall, but to react now would mean almost certain compromise if anyone watched.

All I could do was walk on, turning right at the next intersection, pulling my coat off and running as fast as I could whilst picking out the new streets and judging the right direction to take.

I arrived back at the mall, diving into the first shop on the opposite end from where I'd left. I turned my coat, tucked it in on itself so you couldn't see the dark navy and tried to slow my breath, standing near the air conditioner to cool from the flat-out sprint.

My breath slowed when in through the door she came.

"There you are," she said. "Now I didn't expect to find you in here."

I took my first look at the shelves and tried to hide my alarm as all I saw were lace knickers, long silk basques and in front of me a rainbow of sex toys wrapped in plastic.

"And that's cute," she replied, nodding up to my head. "You're trying to hide yourself. These guys don't care."

I pulled off the cap and let my hair fall to the side, tucking the glasses back in my pocket.

"So what are you after?" a middle-aged assistant said, approaching us.

Alarica turned to look at me in anticipation. "She's shy," she said when I didn't answer.

"Don't be silly," the heavily made up woman said. "We're all adults. Is it something for you or someone else?"

I stood, dumbfounded, unable to speak.

"I'll deal with this," Alarica said. "She's not with anyone at the moment. So something for her."

The assistant's face brightened, ushering me over to a wall covered in long, thick rubber objects more like instruments of torture than pleasure.

"Something small for now," Alarica said, then turned to me. "Start small," she repeated, softer this time and nodded towards the assistant.

13

The day ended with a bag full of Xanax the size of my fist and a stubby pink toy, neither of which Alarica would let me pay for. I'd also made a resolution to run again each day, as I had since I was young. Plus now I had a future source of supply for anything illicit, although the supplier had no idea I might be calling.

From the back of the wardrobe, buried with my cold weather clothes and other things I didn't yet need, I dug out my sports gear the following morning. With the Xanax hidden in a pink sports bottle, I headed out on my first morning run since I'd arrived in this place, timing my departure with the first shards of the light starting across the wide horizon.

With the click of the front door settling back into its space, the rev of Lenart's engine dissipating down the road, it felt so right back in trainers and the familiar feeling of walking on air. I loved the freedom of the loose shorts and thin vest with air rushing past me as I powered between the houses and into the darkness of the canopy, whilst fighting the strain on my lungs I'd let slip out of shape.

Running along the path, I counted a slow rhythm. The five minutes of pumping my legs so hard would have three months ago powered me over a kilometre, but by the panting of my breath this distance would be considerably less.

I stopped, letting my lungs catch as I read the landmarks before fixing on the large oak in the distance, its gnarled branches looking like the fingers of an old man as they spread out. Taking a left, I stepped from the path and over brambles and thickets, fern and foliage for another five minutes. At the base of a distinctive wide tree I could just make out from the path, I buried the contents of the bottle in fallen leaves before retracing my steps.

Arriving back at the house, it would seem I'd been missed, the time longer than I'd intended. The children were already on their way to school, leaving Celina alone in the house. She sat in the living room in her silk gown with a cup of coffee in her hand. Her eyebrow raised as I walked through the door and her comment came as no surprise.

"So you've been getting hot and sweaty without me."

I laughed and ran up the stairs, locking myself away with fresh clothes and a towel. Ignoring the soft knock at the door, I let the water run on as I changed into my morning's clothes.

She sat at the top of the stairs as I opened the door, her face a picture of disappointment when she saw my state of full dress.

"You're no fun," she said and stormed up the next set of stairs.

She came back down within half an hour and stood beside me at the sink, now dressed in a short tennis skirt and a thin white top holding firm against her breasts. Her perfume smelt divine.

"I'm sorry," she said, edging closer. "I'm just a little frustrated at the moment. He's neglecting my needs."

I turned towards her and she spoke again.

"Not that he satisfies them anyway."

Guilt tightened across my chest. It sounded like my plans had been working a little too well for her liking.

Twice Celina had woken in the night to find Lenart still asleep in his chair downstairs. He'd exploded with fury when he woke, venting his mix of the drug-clouded hangover and anger at being left to sleep downstairs.

I vowed to use the same number of tablets on the next bottle, but this time it would be full, so half the potency. The bottle already stood in the cupboard, ready for the first drink to crack the seal so I could add the special ingredient.

"I guess he's just busy at work," I said, drying my hands as the sink drained.

"Ha," she scoffed. "He's a lazy bastard," she replied, then paused. "Sorry I shouldn't speak of him like that." She stopped again. "But he is."

"You're his wife," I replied, closing the door under the sink. "He should be looking after you." For the first time I looked into her damp eyes.

"Yes," she said softly, letting her breath empty, her eyes boring deep into mine. "I'll tell you about that sometime."

"I'm here now," I replied, my words soft, raising my eyebrows in the long pause as I silently urged her to open up.

She'd been hounding me, but for the first time I realised maybe it wasn't for a cheap thrill. Perhaps she wanted a connection, a companion. Someone to be close with.

Taking two steps, I leant forward. She opened her arms and accepted the embrace. Nuzzling her head into my neck, I could feel her tears on my warm skin.

We held as I took a slow deep breath, my shoulders relaxing as tension seemed to flow from us both.

She turned her head, pecking me on the cheek. I twisted toward her and our lips met. Her touch so gentle.

Drawing my head back, I couldn't help but smile and planted my lips to hers again, breathing in gentle peppermint as we opened our mouths still locked together.

Celina leant in with more force and I replied, increasing my pressure against her with our heads angling in opposite directions. Her tongue touched against mine as they swirled together. Feeling her hand move, she stroked down my back, tracing the arch until her palm planted with a firm grip on my ass.

A fire raged inside my stomach. Heat prickled between my legs. Her touch electrified my skin as her hand slipped under my shirt to the small of my back. She pushed in closer. I pushed back, my leg slipping between hers where warmth radiated out like a bonfire.

She let out a groan and pulled her hand around to the front of my bra setting off fireworks as my nipples pushed against her fingers.

I drew back from her embrace, breath panting as I teetered close to diving back in.

My head shook. "No," I said, watching her struggle with her breath, eyes wide and doughy with warmth. Her mouth stood open as if still in the kiss. "I can't. This isn't right."

"Okay," she said, and I blinked at the unexpected answer. "It was wrong of me."

"No. No. It wasn't. I want to. Wow, I really do, but you're married and I'm working. I work for you," I said, stumbling over the words as my body urged every muscle to surge forward and take what I wanted; to dive in feet first and drink down her fruit.

She replied with a sweet smile. "I understand. I shouldn't put you in this situation," she said, her voice low and quiet.

She leant in. This time I kept my head turned away from hers, her breath dancing on my ear as she whispered.

"I'm here if you ever want to."

I pulled back, snatching a peck on her lips and headed from the kitchen, grabbing the keys to the car as I left.

14

I took a right out of the estate, driving at speed past the supermarket and taking little notice of a stream of people heading from a coach into the diner.

On and on I drove, going further than I had before. Mile after mile of empty dry land passed on either side.

Eventually the fire burning within me flickered as it calmed and little by little I let my speed slow.

Before too long I pulled over on to the dirt, but as thoughts began to stir again, I turned the car around.

I was ready for home. Ready to pull on my running gear again and stamp out the rest of my pent-up energy.

Driving back past the diner, the car park around it stood empty apart from the coach I'd seen on the way through. The area around the supermarket was quiet, too, with only the odd car coming or going.

I rolled on at the speed limit for a steady ten minutes more before I felt the tyre go, the car rocking to the side. I manhandled the steering wheel to the right.

Letting the car stumble from the black top and into the dirt, I sat looking along the long stretch of empty road ahead, watching the white lines shimmering in the rising heat haze.

Minutes later, I don't know how long for sure, I left the cool air, letting the heat roll over me. The rim of the wheel rested in the dirt, the tyre with a great split down the side.

Resting my palms on the heat of the roof, I leaned against the metal, staring as the road disappeared on the horizon; the direction of the house. The cloudless sky had barely a breath of wind and for the first time since I'd seen the tall chimney, black, not white smoke pulled high into the air.

Leaving my arms against the heat, I turned in the opposite direction at the sound of air brakes.

The coach from the diner slowed, eventually coming to a stop alongside. I looked along its length and stared for a moment at each face peering back.

The bright-eyed kids smiling in my direction lifted my

mood, as did the women with questioning looks, men with their eyebrows raised. I saw an older child, a teenager, in body at least. She wore a head brace as she smiled wide in my direction with an older woman at her side, wiping dribble from the girl's mouth.

The door of the coach soon swung out and an old man squinted out at me, shouting from the driver's seat.

"Need a hand?" he said in a gruff, low voice which didn't seem to match his smile.

"Thanks, but I think I can manage."

He pushed his hand to his brow, closed the door and the coach moved off.

Within ten minutes I had the car jacked up, sweat beading on my brow as I leant my foot on the wheel brace. The first nut loosened and the brace clattered to the floor. As I stood up, arching my back, I watched as another coach coasted to a stop, this time from the opposite direction.

The window at the driver's side lowered. I half expected it to be the same man. It wasn't, but he gave the same offer.

I declined and he tipped his cap, moving the bus back to the road.

I watched the windows as they sailed past. Each empty, except for the last which had a single pair of eyes glaring in my direction.

In the fleeting view I could see a tall young man with a heavy build who didn't want me looking at him. I watched the coach disappear into the distance, then had the new tyre fitted within another ten minutes.

15

Celina stayed out most of the day, arriving home with the children from school and acting as if the events of the morning had never happened.

More than grateful for her reaction, the week continued in the same vein with neither of us avoiding each other, but her advances had stopped; although I wasn't altogether sure for how long.

The weekend came, and the family trooped off to pick out a dog. Lenart, bleary-eyed, made a point of cutting across Celina as she called an invite to the kitchen.

I was too busy, Lenart added, the place getting in a mess and he took great joy in pointing out the workload would only increase when their new hair-shedding family member joined us.

I wasn't worried about the extra work. I wasn't worried about the not going on the trip. The more time I had to myself, the better; the more time I had to think. To plan. To observe.

Although my manipulation of the situation had been getting results, I felt the process was taking too much time. Each day that went by I felt myself diving more into the detail of the family. The result meant I had to battle off their advances, harmless or not, and I wasn't getting to understand the only snippet of interest from next door.

The space hidden between the study and the bedroom.

In the living room I sat in Lenart's overstuffed leather chair facing the large TV in the corner, with the faces of the street's residents rolling around in my head.

Celina. I'd already discounted her and with the latest insight I firmly relegated her out of contention.

Lenart. I hadn't got into the detail of his life away from the house, but when home, he drank too much, not leaving the house enough to be of any interest. He could be a nine-to-five officer who went to work each day. In intelligence assessment maybe, or some support role, but either way not a risk to me. He also went against the only guidance I'd received which pointed across to the neighbours.

Still, I couldn't fully put him to one side.

Lenara. She seemed like an average housewife, much more so than Celina. She feared her husband straying, but other than the interrogation she'd given, she took no interest in anything and I knew if she hadn't had her condition she wouldn't have taken the help from Alarica.

Frank. Now he was interesting. A doctor, but no longer practicing. Instead, he worked for a corporation in the pharmaceutical industry. He held a thread of interest, despite his charisma overflowing into everyone in his vicinity. He had my attention; so, too, did the room concealed in his study.

A knock at the door interrupted my thoughts and I found Alarica smiling in a short denim skirt and a bright pink vest top leaving little to the imagination as it gave maximum exposure to the sun baking at her back.

Now here stood an interesting character.

A typical early twenties woman. At least what I thought a typical profile would be like. The people I mixed with from an early age were not what you would describe as normal to most.

Alarica loved having an affair with the man of the house. To be honest, who could blame her when he looked like he did, exuding so much charm; if he could do what he'd done to me with one finger...?

I shut down the thought.

She dabbled in drugs, but was smart enough to keep herself safe and no doubt could handle most things thrown at her. She told lies well and could keep a secret. She could act as would be expected of her, putting up such a convincing front. She would say the right things at the right time. With a little training and self-defence lessons, she might even pass selection.

"Night club, next Saturday. You up for it?" she said as the door completed the arc.

My analysis vanished out of my thoughts.

"Ah, yeah," I said, my eyelids batting away my hesitation. "Why not."

"Great."

"Who's coming?" I replied.

"You and me. That enough?" she said, smiling widely.

"Great."

"Catch you later," she said and with that she turned, almost skipping as she headed back to her house.

A club. I hadn't been to one of those for a couple of years. The music had no doubt changed, but it would be nice to get away from this place and let my hair down.

I could feel a smile draw onto my lips. I stiffened them flat, but couldn't hold them from turning back up.

I immediately thought of how I could avoid telling Celina too much of what we planned, in fear that she'd invite herself along. It was the last thing I'd want right now. Instead of a relaxing night with someone who I genuinely enjoyed the company of, I would constantly have to defend myself from her advances, or innuendo, intensifying with each serving of alcohol.

***

It wasn't long before the family were back. No pup bounded out of the car, but their arms were full of supplies and a long list of stores needed next time I went to the shops, all ready for next week and the day when they would pick up the new member of the family.

I avoided any looks from Lenart and busied myself with the day until it was time for Alarica to call, but she didn't. Instead, I called at the house to find it locked up, the dog gone too, if the lack of a barked reply from the doorbell was anything to go by.

Heading home whilst trying to put the question of why Alarica had mentioned nothing, I changed into my running gear before heading between the houses to sprint along the hard-baked mud path, savouring the cool air as I passed under the thick canopy.

I ran for ten minutes, letting my mind clear, focusing on the details of the path ahead and the trees either side whilst keeping my breath even so I could listen to the noises of the forest; the birds singing and the small creatures scurrying from each of my footfalls and other strange sounds which I couldn't quite put my fingers on.

I ran on for another ten minutes before letting myself slow, stopping to lean against a tree to allow my breathing to calm. My head had cleared by this time, my thoughts turning to how the hell I'd get a look in the hidden room and see what was in there.

Could it just be a safe to keep the family jewels in?

If Frank could afford the house, then he could well have pots of money or gold he didn't trust to the banks.

Could it be a deep wardrobe? But then why build it in a study at all? Why not extend the other way, widening the one in the bedroom?

Hadn't they just had the whole place gutted and the inside rebuilt?

A sex dungeon? I'd read in some book I'd long forgotten the title of, but surely Alarica would know about it, either now or soon. She would have said something.

Perhaps something more mundane.

A room with CCTV monitors. Part of a comprehensive security system. Although I'd seen no sign of any camera, inside or out.

Perhaps it held computers, a server maybe? Locked away and sound-proofed, but then wouldn't it need an air conditioner? The condenser obvious outside from some angle?

It wasn't large enough to be a space to relax in and he had his study for that. It was too small for a gym and why keep it locked?

Maybe it housed some specialist equipment. Maybe he was a scuba diver or had some other unique hobby. Of course it could be a deep wardrobe and used for storage, the ornate doors just a way of hiding its mundane nature.

Realising my pace had slowed, my thoughts paused as I concentrated on a sound alien to the forest. A sound I knew, but was out of place.

About to run again I stopped as Alarica joined the path just a few steps in front, her cheeks flushed, her face a picture of alarm with her head flashing back from where she'd stepped from.

I followed her look but a thick tree obscured the sight, then watched her double take back to me, a grin appearing as she realised who'd startled her.

About to bound forward to ask what she was up to, I stopped as another leg stepped from behind the tree and on to the path.

Frank. Behind him, the dog bounded over, his lead held at Frank's wrist. With red cheeks and tired eyes, Frank looked like he'd just been running too.

"Bloody shit ran off after a rabbit," he blurted, turning to me with concern.

Alarica burst into laughter, wiping her mouth with the back of her hand.

"What?" Frank replied with a nervous laugh.

"This is Catarina," she replied. "Remember her? She's that one. Rein," she added, tipping her head in my direction.

"Oh yes," Frank replied, his mouth beaming wide. "Sorry, Catarina, I didn't recognise you without the dress." He held his hand out, taking two steps forward.

I held my palm up. "I'm all sweaty," I said.

"That doesn't bother me," he replied, taking my hand and kissing the back of it.

"Nice to see you both, but I better finish my run," I said, and without giving a chance for reply I ran past them, catching a few words from Alarica before the distance built.

"I'll ask her."

16

I'm in a stranger's room.

A strange room.

The moonlight is shining from the wrong place. That's not my window.

My head hurts as I squint around.

Have they drugged me?

It's a similar feeling, but not quite the same as I've felt before.

There's a SIG Sauer P226 on the side. Or a hairbrush and a comb at an unlucky angle.

I'm naked.

No. There's a long t-shirt there, or a nightie. I don't own a nightie.

I can see the white of my smalls discarded to the side of the bed. I'm not alone according to the soft snore at my side.

My throat is hoarse. I ache all over.

The night started out in the city. A cab ride for about an hour. A bar, another bar soon after.

Talking about everything and nothing with Alarica. Ally after last night and she calls me Rein, or Cat now.

It sounded best when she said it with her German accent. Clean. Pure. I don't feel like that now.

We talked about the job, which she showed so much enthusiasm for.

No plans to move on in the immediate future. There's talk of her joining Frank's firm later on, when she's ready for a more serious job.

She directed the same question to me.

I told her I wasn't looking, but things always change. I didn't want to be cleaning houses all my life. I have skills, I remember saying. She laughed in reply, then asked what skills I had.

I can't remember my response, just a vague recollection I'd drawn the conversation back to her, over and again, veering from my backstory where the danger grew more real as each of the drinks flooded my brain.

I wished for the pills they'd mentioned in training to slow the effect of alcohol. But I'm alone; their stark reply reaffirming each time.

Four or five drinks in, I let loose. Egged on by her enthusiasm, matching her pace and she can drink.

Men formed up, strutting like peacocks, a queue stretching out till we moved on again.

The club. Some small place, famous in the area, but only by those in the know. Busy, but not packed. Loud, but still we could hear. Invited by a stranger to the VIP area where they left us alone.

She had me drink all sorts. Drinks of all colours. Smells and tastes I'd never seen.

I slowed several times only for her to speed me up as we slipped back into our flow.

She started with her challenge again, to get me to lose what I hadn't already; the conversation as clear as if it had been just moments ago. I repeated I wasn't in a rush.

I should be, she'd said. It would open my eyes. I told her for the first time about how I almost did with Celina. I told how much I'd wanted to, would have, if the situation had been different.

She said it wouldn't matter; it's different with a man. Not better, but different.

I told her I was happy to wait for the right one.

She turned to point around the small area. "Which one?" she'd said, her finger outstretched to each man in turn.

"Not a stranger," I'd said.

"Who then?" she asked, another drink in our hands, my laughter rising. "What about Frank?" she'd said, her eyebrows raised when I didn't reply.

"He's for someone else," I said after a pause.

She smiled. "What if I didn't mind?" she'd replied.

What if his wife did? I recalled not mentioning.

"Do you fancy him?" she asked.

I remember the long pause before my reply. "What's not to like?"

"Then why not?"

"He probably wouldn't even want to," I replied, doing my best to stop the giggle.

She shot back, "He does. He asked me to tell you."

"Tell me what?" I replied, my smile beaming as I felt the nerves rise.

"That he wants you. He wants to fuck you. He told me."

I'd sat back in the seat, staring at her. I remember the shock even though I shouldn't have been surprised.

"He told you he wants to fuck me?" I said. I remember the slur in my voice.

"Yes, he wants to be your first," she'd replied.

"You told him? How does that even come up?" I asked, almost shrieking, another full glass in my hand from nowhere.

She smiled and let the silence hang.

"And you don't mind?" I'd asked.

"No," she replied without pause. "My present to you." Silence hung again between us, only the beat of the bass in the air.

"I'd be too nervous," I said.

"Don't be. You won't be," she said.

"Why?" I replied.

A smile grew on her face as she wet her lips with her tongue. "I'll be there to hold your hand," she said, letting her eyebrows rise and fall.

"You like to watch?" I said, my voice just above the pounding beat.

"More than watching," she replied, leaning forward to let her breasts swell over the line of her low-cut dress.

I drew my gaze from the table line and took a deep breath, swallowing a large mouthful of champagne.

"Hell, why not?" I said, and we both burst into a fit of laughter.

Another bottle arrived. We were still laughing as the

cork shot over the balcony and on to the teeming dance floor.

The bottle finished too soon. The night dimmed in my mind. We hardly spoke on the cab ride home, both sleepy, hands held as we leant against each other, rousing only when the driver spoke.

No payment necessary. Pre-booked and paid.

I was in her bed, the rest of the night clearing. We'd padded up the stairs, no questions asked, no glance over to the house. My current home.

We drank water in the darkened, silent kitchen. Closed the bedroom door, watched as we took turns to undress in the soft lamp light. I pulled on a borrowed nightie and slipped into bed. A peck on the lips.

I remember asking if she knew how to do that thing he did, but sleep came before she tried to answer.

Panic drained. My eyes rested on the comb and hairbrush at a right angle and I let myself drift back to the darkness.

17

The next time I woke, light poured into the room. Alarica, Ally, sat up next to me with a book in her hands. One of my favourites of Lee Child's. She put it down as she saw me rouse.

"Good morning," she said. "How's the head?"

"Not bad, better than it was in the night."

"What a night," she exclaimed. I nodded, wiping my hands over my face.

"To be repeated," I replied.

"Soon," she said; no mention made of my agreement to her proposal. No comment. No wink or nudge. She was all talk and bluster.

I felt the relief as I changed into a pair of borrowed jeans and a loose t-shirt and headed downstairs, aiming for the door, but not making it before Lenara called my name.

"Join us for breakfast," she said, no room in her voice for a negative response.

I turned and saw the children sat one either side, the table set for six with three spaces. One I filled, the other at my side grabbed by Ally.

I ate eggs and toast as quick as I could between the small talk; the causal chat about our night out.

My heart jumped as the front door closed. I looked at Ally, who hadn't even flinched. Frank came in moments later, dropping the Sunday papers in the middle of the table, complaining about the queue at the shop.

He said hello as if in surprise at my presence and waved a good morning to Ally.

Within ten minutes I was out of the door, the food fighting to stay in place because of the speed I'd forced it down and the obstinance of my stomach to take on anything more than a few sips of water. I'd survived the breakfast with no funny looks from Frank or Ally, especially pleased I'd had none from Lenara. I pushed the memories of the night to the back of my mind.

I returned to the house, grateful to find it empty and

soon remembered today was the day of the new family member's arrival.

I forced myself into my running gear. I had to clear my head.

After dumping the breakfast and the last of last night's drinks a mile or so into the woods, I felt on the way to humanity.

Another four miles and a long hot shower and I resembled a human again, just in time for the arrival of the three excited new parents and a dog the size of a baby leaving a trail of piss on the wooden floor as it explored its new home.

Lenart's eyes fixed on me as he issued his unvoiced command.

After an hour of following in its wake, the new pup settled down on the sofa with the children, the most I'd seen the siblings together in the main part of the house in the weeks before.

The next day, the dog found his name, Fuzz, because of the lay of its hair, the tight curls which would flatten out as it grew.

The week felt as if I was looking after a toddler. Celina helped, but she was no good with clearing up the mess and would get so excited about Fuzz's cuteness she'd forget all the important things, like keeping things out of its reach and making sure they regularly fed it.

I think I enjoyed that time, helped because my relationship with Celina had changed. Previously I'd felt like prey stalked by a wild tiger; now we got along more like women of the same age.

Despite being more reserved than Ally, our connection grew. I found her alone the following Friday after lunch, the kids staying away and Lenart out until late for drinks with people from his company.

I joined at her side, a bottle of wine and two glasses in my hands. Her questioning the sanity of the idea showed how much our relationship had evolved.

"Are you sure?" she said.

"It's a Wednesday," I replied, and she took the glass without a word, instead sharing sight of the puppy as he harassed Brad, snapping at the hoe. Brad seemed to be enjoying himself as much as Fuzz, especially with us both watching.

With the second glass and at Brad's departure, we talked. Celina asked about my night out, her shoulders leaning forward as I told her how much fun we'd had.

With the second bottle and the third glass, I couldn't help but invite her along when we next went out.

With the words her manner changed. Her smile softened as she sat back into the bench.

"That's very sweet of you, but I can't do that," she replied.

"You can. I'm inviting you," I said; I couldn't help thinking she was trying to make me beg.

"I've got responsibilities here," she said. "I'm married."

I laughed. I couldn't help it.

She looked up.

"I don't understand."

"No you don't, but you don't need to," she replied, finishing up her glass and topping us both up.

This was interesting. I thought she would have jumped at the chance, but now she was backing down.

"I wouldn't enjoy it, anyway."

"Don't give me that rubbish," I said, my voice raising. "You can't go out because of your husband?"

Celina paused for a long while before she answered. "Yes, and my responsibilities to this," she said, looking all around.

"What about his responsibilities?" I said, feeling my anger building. "Doesn't he have responsibilities to you?"

"You don't understand what I mean," she said. "I just can't do that."

"Okay, but I'll say this then I'll get on. You've got a messed-up set of priorities somewhere. You married him, you took on his kids, cutting off your youth prematurely. You've been trying to fuck me since I've arrived and now you're saying that you can't go out with me as a friend to have some fun for one night?" I shook my head. "I don't get it."

I stood and turned to leave. Glancing back, I half expected her to be in tears, but she just looked up at me with a neutral expression and the glass empty in her hand.

***

We didn't cross paths until later the next day. She called me from downstairs, shouting up about a hand-delivered package.

As I walked down the stairs, I heard the door click closed and her car start, the engine noise disappearing out into the open.

My gaze fell to a beautiful cream box about the size of a telephone directory sat on the phone stand in the hallway. Tied to the box with a peach ribbon, a bow on top, sat a small white rectangle of card with my name written in a swirl of ink.

I took the box and climbed the stairs, holding it as if there could be anything inside. Arriving in my room, I'd already ruled out explosives; too light and it gave off no odour other than a delicate musk of perfume.

The contents didn't move as I rocked it from side to side. I sat on the edge of my bed, looking all around, expecting some great surprise as I pulled both ends of the bow.

There was no hiss of escaping gas. No cloud of powder pluming from behind the neat lines of the box. Instead, just the faint crinkle of tissue paper covering the contents. Placing the lid with care at my side, I lifted the delicate paper to find a note written by a curve-perfect hand.

Not looking beyond, I read:

My Dear Cat,

Saturday is the night. Be around mine at 6pm. Bring an overnight bag, you won't be back till the morning.

Wear something short, cut low and heels. In the box are some nice things from a mutual friend who can't wait to see what they look like on the floor.

Excitedly,

A xx

Oh, shit.

It hadn't been the drink talking.

She'd actually gone through with it. It wasn't an elaborate joke.

Even though I knew it's what she'd been angling at all this time, and pretending to go through with it was the only option I could think of for getting into the centre room, now she'd arranged the deed I felt a nervousness I hadn't felt since my first days on the pommel horse.

After all I'd gone through. My first experiences of Welbeck. The pain and fear of selection. The hidden objective. The attrition and aggressive pace of training and what happened after, stood naked taking two lives. Still, the thought of what they had planned for me made me barely able to stand with fear, my vision almost blurring to black as I pulled up the tissue paper again and saw the near see-through white silk edged in lace.

Closing the lid I set the box to the side, not able to pull out the soft garments for fear I'd faint.

I sat on the bed, not moving, taking slow, deliberate breaths for what seemed like an age, but was probably just a matter of minutes. I looked to the box and at my reflection in the tall mirror beside the dresser.

After a moment I stood and slowly stripped down until naked.

My gaze hovered over my reflection and I smiled. Turning to the box I leant towards it, but just as I was about to touch the sleek lines I changed my mind and swapped into my shorts and sports bra.

I ran for longer than I'd expected. Struggling to get my bearings as I ran back, I had to get to the edge of the woods, turning back and counting in my head.

The process worked and I was at my tree within ten minutes, back and in the shower within another fifteen.

Not alone in the house anymore, it gave me reason to hide the box away in the wardrobe without exploring its contents.

Distracted, I went about the next couple of days. Alarica didn't call, and I walked the dog with just the children.

18

The next day I headed to town, my first excursion in the daylight since this area had become my home.

I had nothing resembling short, other than my running gear. Nothing cut low enough for Ally's request. I've never owned a tall heel.

Combining a few of Celina's requests, I took the car for the drive to the town where we'd spent those few hours drinking.

I chose a department store similar to one I would have used at home, expecting they'd have all I needed. For once I was trying to dress my age and gender, not that of ten or twenty years older, usually trying to hide every aspect which differentiated the sexes.

Despite their vast range, they had nothing close to what I needed and I ended up buying three choices for each of the categories; each of the nine items from different shops. For the first time I said things to myself others had said when I'd been forced to shop with them.

In the end, I left satisfied with my decisions, knowing at least one of each choice should work whilst berating myself for even caring.

I wrapped up Celina's small purchases and stopped at the post office, purchasing a pen, some tape and a small postal box. I discarded the pen and the tape after I sealed the box and addressed it. With my shopping back in the car I headed to the stout five-storey building a short walk from the main high street.

Let in by a tall man dressed in a crease-free suit who grinned as he held the door wide, I thanked him without locking eyes, following the signs to the reception where I found a middle-aged woman behind a desk. Her face looked like she kept the major cosmetic companies in business single-handed.

"Package for Mr Rozman," I said in a forthright voice, placing the package on the desk between us.

The woman behind the counter raised her eyebrows, tipping her head to the side. "No Mr Rozman here, my love," she said, widening her eyes.

I turned the parcel around with the address facing me and took time to read it back.

"Is the address correct?" I said, turning it in her direction.

She nodded after I'd watched her scan the words.

"So no Lenart Rozman?"

"No, I would know him. There's only about a hundred people in the building and I know them all by name," she said, her gaze wandering up to the ceiling in thought. "But hang on, let me check. He may be a new starter, but then again I do the inductions so that won't be right."

Still she tapped her chubby fingers on the keyboard out in front of her, her eyes set on the screen below the counter top.

Her face lit up after a few seconds. "Well I don't know," she said with surprise, her eyes widening so much I could see cracks appear in her thick foundation. "We have a Lenart Rozman, up on floor three." Her voice slowed. "He must use one of the hot desks." She took the parcel and placed it on the floor by her feet, her eyelids batting the thick false lashes together as she barely noticed me say goodbye.

Now I had the information I needed.

This place was a front.

Lenart Rozman was a someone.

I'd been told to concentrate on fifty-six, which meant either they were wrong or he was unconnected and this was something I alone could use.

Grinning widely, I headed back to the car.

19

By Saturday morning the dog's novelty was wearing thin with the family so I walked the woods with just my thoughts and the fuzzball for company. The afternoon came too soon and I busied myself doing what I thought someone in my situation should do.

I took a long bath, shaved and tidied, washed my hair and preened and plucked where I had never preened and plucked before. I took time to dry before covering in a towelling robe to make the short journey to my room. Hesitantly, I slid the bolt and pulled the handle, preparing for who could be standing the other side of the door.

"Catarina," Celina said in a quiet voice. "Lenart wants me to ask you where you're going tonight. To make sure you're safe."

"Hi, Celina. How are you doing?" I replied.

"I'm fine," she said, her tone flat, gaze turning down the stairs.

"I'm staying next door," I replied with a large smile. "And I've got to get ready," I added, already shuffling along the corridor before pushing the door closed at my back.

I let my anger evaporate with two long deep breaths. The controlling bastard downstairs should be asleep by now. I waited until I heard footsteps headed down the stairs before I removed my robe.

After hanging the gown on the back of the door, I hesitated, my hands lingering on the handles of the wardrobe.

I didn't believe in anything I couldn't see, couldn't touch, but in that moment I knew the next few hours, the next few days, had a weight I was only just beginning to realise.

Shaking off the thought, I pulled the off-white box from its hiding place and laid it on the bed, where it sat as I stared, hoping for new-found courage. More than a minute passed before I told myself how stupid I was being and pulled up the lid, taking the note and reading it three times over before setting it to the side.

Removing the final layer of paper, I stared at the thin pair of white knickers, my fingers reaching out to touch at the silk and trace the beautiful lace edge before pulling them from the box.

A matching bra sat underneath, with cups of the same thin material, again edged with the fine lace finish.

Standing, I slipped them on and turned to the mirror. A perfect fit.

My mouth moved of its own accord and I caught myself smiling back. They were a beautiful gift, the fit so comfortable I could barely feel them against my skin.

Letting my gaze wander, I circled the contrast of my areola, just visible as my nipples gave their own opinion, my look drifting to the thin strip of hair I could just make out between my legs.

I turned away, taking several deep breaths and pulled on a tight yellow vest top, wrapping the tops of my thighs in a thin black skirt.

I couldn't help but smile back in the mirror, drawing myself away, shaking my head, soon pulling a heavy coat over my shoulders, thankful its drop was so much longer than the clothes I was just about wearing.

With the briefest of goodbyes and my small overnight bag in my hand, I opened the door into the warm night air, pausing only briefly as I saw six cars bumper to bumper and side to side in fifty-six's driveway.

For a moment I wondered if there would be an audience.

The door opened after a short wait. It was Lenara. I let the breath catch in my chest.

"Come in," she said. "Don't just stand there."

I took a tentative step, letting my gaze pass over new plasters on each of her thumbs before moving to the side to let her push the door shut.

I heard a rabble of gossiping voices from the living room. All women. Not a team event, surely?

"Come and meet everyone," Lenara said, ushering me

out of the hall.

In the living room I forced my eyes not to widen as I saw seven middle-aged women turning with a smile at my entrance.

"Ladies. This is their lady from next door. Catarina." The group erupted with a series of hellos and raised glasses in my direction.

Following the welcomes around the room, I searched out a friendly face whilst hoping Frank wasn't among them. Before I could finish my greetings, a double blast of a car horn sounded from outside and the stairs lit up with the pound of rushing feet, Ally soon beaming at the door, followed by a gentle breeze of her sweet perfume.

Also draped in a long coat, she grabbed me by the arm, shouting a goodbye, dragging me out of the door and toward a large Mercedes parked at the curb, the rear door held wide by a silver-haired man in a black suit.

After handing over our bags and taking a seat on the deep leather beside her, Ally grabbed me by the shoulders and squeezed me in a tight embrace.

"You excited?" she said, not able to hide her own joy.

"Of course," I replied, a real smile fixed on my face. "But I thought we were going to..." I paused, not sure of the words. "...Be at your place?"

"Oh no. Not at the house. No."

"I thought Lenara and the kids would have been out. Wouldn't we be more comfortable there?"

"No. Not at the house," she insisted. "Anyway, you haven't seen where we're going."

"Can you imagine what I thought as I saw all those old women in the front room?" I said, not needing to feign the shock.

Ally burst out in a howl of laughter and it soon dawned on me that I needed a change of plan.

I only agreed to the situation thinking I'd just be going through the motions to get them alone in the house, get them in a state where I could find out more about that room and somehow see if it was safe to access. But now that approach was out of the question. We were going somewhere out of my control and I had to figure out how the hell I'd get out of what they had planned for me.

"Where are we going?" I said, waiting for when I knew my voice would sound calm.

"An amazing hotel, well out of the way."

"You've been there before?" I said.

A grin came back in reply. "Settle back, you look so nervous."

She was right and now I had every right to be, but I did as she said and settled into the seat, watching her open a compartment at our feet and pull out a bottle of champagne, condensation dripping to the carpet.

We drank whilst keeping the conversation light, talking about anything other than what we were in for. Then, without warning, she paused and turned my way, her face wide with alarm.

"You are wearing them, aren't you?"

A grin launched to my face without my control. "I am."

Her tension disappeared as quickly as it had come. "Don't they feel so amazing?" she said.

I agreed and told her they fit so well.

"One of those things I can do," she replied, raising her eyebrows before returning the conversation back to yesterday's shopping trip.

Time raced by the darkened windows, as it always seemed to in Ally's company, and before I'd fully prepared my nerves, we pulled up under the canopy of a hotel.

The door opened soon after, with our bags handed off to a waiting porter.

I stepped out wide-eyed, taking in the entrance bathed in golden light. Ally linked her arm in mine. Our heels clicked across the stone floor as the tall maître d' showed us to the bar.

"He'll be finishing up in the next half hour," Ally said, tipping her head across the wide reception.

I followed her look and peered through the open restaurant door. Frank sat at a table with his side to us.

If he'd seen us arrive he didn't let on. He laughed as he ate, talking with a short fat man whose hands gesticulated out in front of his face.

"Business," she said, as she turned to the barman, ordering a bottle of champagne whilst taking off her coat and handing it to a porter who'd appeared at our side.

My jaw almost dropped to see her outfit was a near match for my own; her black skirt maybe just a little shorter, the line of her top sweeping much lower than I'd dared.

She smirked in my direction as I stared back at her tilted-head question.

"Your coat?" she said, smiling. "Come on. You can't wear that all night. Let's have a look at you."

I peeled off the coat and handed it to the uniformed man at my side, soon aware of the sharp conditioned air giving me a sense of how few clothes I wore.

Ally surveyed me from head to foot with her eyebrows raised. I'm sure it was the dry air that made her lick her lips.

With care I raised myself up to sit on the bar stool, trying my best not to expose the expensive lingerie barely masking what waited underneath. Taking up a glass, I clinked it with Ally's as she offered.

With each mouthful I relaxed a little more, our conversation only tempered by being in a public location, although the lounge populated with only the odd group here and there; a few businessmen gathered around drinks and two guys in sharp suits who seemed out of place, each sitting alone with their backs to the bar.

Using the mirror as I chatted, I kept glancing over, watching as they continually scanned the room. Not overt, but because of my nature and training, it was more than obvious.

As I observed between Ally's flow of conversation, I noticed although both were wearing different suits, their builds different, each jacket had been tailored oversized.

It could only mean one of a few things;

they'd both lost weight, although their trousers seemed right; they both had the same tailor who liked to give a little space for growth, or they were trying to hide something.

My pessimistic mind drew the latter conclusion and assumed the space would be for a handgun.

Before I could make any more observations, I caught the sound of Frank's voice booming a goodbye.

I turned, watching him in the mirror as he shook the fat guy's hand before hugging him, then holding his palm out in a stationary wave as the guy walked behind us. I caught sight in the bar's mirror of a glance in our direction, the fat guy taking in the view of our pair of asses.

I turned, forcing my knees together. Ally followed, hers not so tightly pressed.

Frank greeted us at the bar, soon presented with a drink with no one asking.

"Great to see you, Al," he said. "You look beautiful as always," he added, leaning forward and giving her a lingering peck on the cheek as he held her bare shoulders.

Both turned in my direction, Frank's smile almost as wide as Ally's. "And Catarina, so amazing you could make it. We're going to have such a great time on this momentous occasion."

I thought for a moment on his words as he walked the two steps in my direction, then realised what he was referring to.

His hands were huge and warm on the tops of my bare arms, his touch stealing my breath as we both leant forward. I could hear him taking a slow deep breath as his face came closer, eventually planting his lips on my cheek. With my head beside his I saw another man whose jacket hung too large, following some way behind Frank from the restaurant.

"Come. Let's sit down," Frank said as he ushered us towards a round lounge chair.

"Let's just go upstairs," Ally announced with a high-pitched tone and gesturing with her hands towards the lift, barely keeping the champagne within the glass.

"Al," Frank said, raising his eyebrows in her direction. "I know you've been looking forward to this, but why don't we savour the moment? Take some time to get acquainted."

I smiled as he lingered in my direction.

"Don't you think, Cat? I hope you don't mind if I call you Cat?"

"Of course I don't," I replied, feeling calmer with each of his words as my voice slowed. "I want to get to know the man who's going to be the special one." I couldn't believe I'd just said those words.

I watched on with the breath caught in my lungs as I saw his Adam's apple rise and fall whilst he took a deep draw.

"Great, let's sit down and get some refreshment."

As he turned, I spoke again.

"I'm just going to use the bathroom first."

He gave a corner-mouth smile in reply as I took care over each step, heading the short walk across the foyer, hearing Ally's excited whispers as I pushed the heavy door and took refuge in a stall.

They'd taken my coat and with it the tablet-lined pocket.

Racing through what I should do next, all I could come up with was the hope I'd find it in the room with the bags; the room where the deed was going to happen. I'd have to slip them into their drinks and buy myself time for the effect.

Everything had complicated with the one simple act and I racked my brains to figure out how I could hope to get out of this whole disaster.

Could I feign illness?

Could I say I wasn't ready?

Too nervous?

Something unexpected had come up?

My thoughts crashed to a halt as a loud bang rang from the foyer. A sound I was all too familiar with. A sound I knew could only be a gun shot.

20

With barely a thought I jumped from the stall, wrapping my fingers around the handle and wrestling the heavy washroom door open. To screams in the background, at arm's reach, a bald, fat guy in a cheap black suit stood waving a pistol across my view as he screamed rushed commands into the frantic room.

I'd soon figured his lack of skill when he still hadn't seen me by the time I'd taken in the room's detail, the most important of which was the gun pointed in Ally's direction as she shielded Frank for the second time since we'd met.

Time didn't slow like they say in the movies; my reactions were instant. Simultaneously, I pushed out my palms with the right just ahead to catch the hot barrel of the Ruger GP100 six shooter, my left balled, smacking at his wrist. It didn't land as well as I'd hoped, but punched with enough force for the intended effect.

The guy turned, his sagging jowls following, but too late to prevent what would come next. With his left hand empty, as now was his right, the gun passed by the hot barrel from my right hand to my left whilst tracking down the length of his leg, stopping only a fraction of a second before I blew a wide hole in his foot.

As his foot exploded, his fists unclenched and with a high scream he collapsed to the floor with his hands reaching out to clutch what remained.

I took a step back, the washroom door cold on my upper arms as two of the bodyguards rounded with their SIG Sauers trained at his mass, their eyes flitting between the wounded man and the gun in my hand.

Ally ran over, dragging me away, her palm out to the men, making it clear I was on their side. Frank had disappeared. In the corner of my vision I'd seen one of his men pushing him past a shattered mirror and into the restaurant.

Ally took the gun from my loose grip, her thumb

flicking the safety before placing it on a nearby table.

"You okay?" she said with her warm hands rubbing up and down my upper arms.

I waited to answer, pulling in a deep breath I didn't need to take.

"What just happened?" I said, forcing myself to gulp at the air.

"That man tried to kill Frank."

"Oh my god. Is he all right?" I replied, letting my tone rise.

"He is because of you, but we'd better get out of here."

Ally called over to the nearest guy in an over-sized suit jacket.

"Get the car out front," she said, her tone sterner than I'd heard before, even when chastising the Bukia's kids. The guy didn't question the command, instead nodding as he spoke into his cuff whilst walking away to help his colleague search the crumpled mass on the floor.

We were out of the hotel in less than a minute. Out of town in another ten, speeding down a long lonely road with Ally's arms surrounding my cold shoulders.

"What was all that about?" I ventured.

Ally pulled herself back upright and leant forward to a compartment where she pulled out a metal hip flask. Unscrewing the top, she took a swig before offering it over.

"It'll help with the shock," she said, and I let her place it in my hand.

The liquid bit at the back of my throat, vapours reaching up to my sinus, turning to warmth as it travelled down. I took another and turned, waiting for the answer.

For over a minute I watched her think, watched her expression change as she planned, checking over what she was about to say. "Frank is a very important man. He has influences all over the world. His company has enemies."

"Enemies? Is this the first time someone has tried to kill him?"

"No, not the first. There are people who don't like what

he does. What his company does."

"Hence the bodyguards."

"He'll be getting new ones real soon," she said, pausing with her mouth open, apparently unsure if she should voice what waited on the tip of her tongue.

"What does he do that's so bad?" I replied.

"Nothing," she snapped back.

"Sorry, I didn't mean it like that, but someone must think it's bad. You just said so," I said, holding my hands up to her.

"No, I'm sorry," she said and leant forward, holding me in a tight embrace. Still clutching my upper arms, she spoke quietly at my ear. "Some people want a piece of him, like he has a value. Some people want him to stop what he's doing so they can carry on making money. If he succeeds, then he'll put many people out of business. But enough of that," she said, pulling out of the embrace. "Now it's your turn," she said, raising her eyebrows.

"What?" I replied, doing my best to feign surprise.

"How did you learn to do that?" she replied, her eyebrows still high on her forehead.

"Do what?"

"Don't be coy." The softness had disappeared from her words and I knew I couldn't act this out forever.

"My dad was in the RAF. When he heard where I was going he made me take self-defence classes. Two solid weeks of training."

"With guns?" she said, her voice rising as her eyebrows relaxed.

"He knows they're everywhere here, so he insisted I knew how to handle anything I came across."

"But still those were some amazing moves. I saw everything. You didn't even pause for thought. That guy went down as soon as you were out of the bathroom."

"Am I going to get in trouble for shooting him? Will the police be after me?" I said, letting myself shrink back into the seat.

Ally's arm appeared on my shoulder and she drew me close. "No. Frank will see to that," she said, letting me go. "I don't understand how you could train with guns in the UK. Your laws are so rigid."

"My dad pulled a few strings. He used to be in some cross-service group and got a couple of his friends still in the army to give me the training."

"What unit?"

"I'm not sure. SES or something?"

"The SAS?"

"Yeah, that sounds about right. I think they specialise in jumping out of planes or something. Nice guys though and seemed to know what they were talking about."

Ally laughed as I knew she would and she seemed happy to accept my story, for now at least, pushing the hip flask towards my left hand. I accepted the whiskey again, taking it with my right.

"Are you left-handed?" she said as she watched me drink.

"No," I replied with a frown, until I realised the reason for the question. "They taught me ambidextrously. I'm much better with my right, but there's not always enough time to do it that way, they would say, and they were correct."

"Wow," she said. "I..." she added, but stopped herself saying any more.

"And you seemed to know a thing or two yourself. You flipped the gun to safe like you've handled before."

She burst out laughing and I realised the innuendo.

"I've handled a few before," she said as she calmed. "No seriously, my dad took me to the range since I was young. He too was in the military."

I knew that was likely to be a lie. The gun laws in Germany were almost as restrictive as at home.

"Where are we going?" I said, even though I knew we were on the road home.

"Home. I think it best, don't you? We must reconvene soon though, but that kind of killed the mood," she said as she laughed.

"Shall we have a drink first?" I ventured, too wired to go back to the Rozman's to sleep. "Please?"

"An amazing idea," she replied and leant forward to the driver, speaking quietly.

Soon we arrived at the next town, still half an hour away from home. We stopped outside a small bar and the driver pulled open the door.

It was still early in the evening and the bar sat quiet. Only when all the eyes in the room stared in our direction, the men's tongues rolling out onto the table and the women's eyes squinting, I remembered how little I wore.

I tried to mimic Ally's confident trot to the bar and we ordered from the short cocktail menu, finding a booth by the window before sidling up close to each other so we could talk quietly.

"How are you getting on with Celina and Lenart now?"

"Fine, I think. Celina has backed off. I might have seen the real side of her now. She's lonely in that house and not happy with Lenart, that's obvious."

"That pig. There's something odd about him."

"Apart from being a dirty old man?"

"Most are dirty old men at heart, aren't they?" she said, and we burst into laughter, a repeat of the drinks arriving at the table unasked for. The barman pointed to a group of four twenty-something men who looked over. Renewing our laughter, we toasted in their direction, shaking our heads as they stood.

"He's odd though," she said. "I mean, he's a nosey fucker. I've seen him in his garden looking up at the house. Nothing too obvious. He's usually doing something else, but seeming to always keep glancing up towards us."

"Maybe he's hoping to catch you naked? Or Lenara?"

Laughter burst out again.

"I'm sure he's harmless, but he gives me the creeps. When the builders had the place, they said he came around several times asking questions about what they were doing."

"Why would he be interested?"

"I don't know. It was nothing more interesting than a remodel," she replied. "It must have been bad because otherwise the builders wouldn't have said anything. He was asking what the materials were for."

"What do you mean?" I replied, trying to hold back my enthusiasm for where this was leading.

"I'm no builder," she said, and I tilted my head to the side.

"Really?" I replied, grinning.

Ally put her hand on my bare knee and with a sharp look she told me to stop being silly. My breath caught until she moved her hand back to her drink.

"When they were loading dry wall into the house," she said.

I interrupted again. "What's dry wall?"

She grinned and shook her head. "They make new walls with it. I think it's plaster."

"Oh, plasterboard. Got you," I replied, nodding.

"He was asking so many questions."

"Nosey bastard."

"Yeah. Keep an eye on him. I wouldn't put it past him to have a camera in your room," she said.

I shook off the shiver as it ran down my spine.

"Or in your bathroom."

"Don't say that. Oh my god."

"But I guess you can't blame him," she said, looking me up and down.

"Stop it. I won't be able to sleep now."

"Don't worry, you can sleep with me from now on," she said, and we both gave a hollow laugh as we turned back to our drinks.

After another five or six rounds, I can't remember the exact count, the talk had grown louder and left us breathless with laughter.

"I'm really sorry about tonight," she said, her bare leg touching against mine as if she was trying to get closer. "I hope it hasn't put you off trying again?"

I paused, filling the moment with a large swallow of bright-coloured liquid.

"Of course not. My life is frustration."

She grinned. "You better stay at mine tonight. The Rozman's aren't expecting you back."

I smiled with a shallow nod so the room wouldn't spin too much.

The car had been waiting outside all the while and the journey home flashed by as we continued to chat about so much of nothing. In a rare pause for breath I couldn't help reflecting on what had been a great night, a great day..

I'd handled a gun, something I'd been used to doing daily for so long. I flexed my instincts, although not by choice. I had great company and I wasn't unhappy about the attention I'd been getting in my nearly not-there clothes. So many times I'd nearly forgotten I was working, reminding myself to focus and keep control, then Ally would say something funny and I'd forget myself again.

Arriving back, the houses were in darkness. The driver waited until we were through the door, then with bottles of water we were straight up to her room.

"I'll need to borrow something again. We left our bags at the hotel," I said. "Or do I?" I added, pulling off the top to reveal the thin silk bra.

She blew out a deep breath and smiled back, handing me a nightie from the dresser and grabbing her own before heading out of the door.

I'd changed by the time she'd arrived back in her nightie. "Have you gone all shy on me?" I said, covering my mouth as the words slurred.

"Of course not," she said, stepping close, cupping her hand on my cheek. "I just don't want to spoil the surprise when we finally get the night."

I let my smile turn to a grin and I headed to the bathroom, soon returning to find her wrapped up in the covers, the main light off, the lamp at her bedside providing the warm glow.

As I pulled myself under the covers, she turned and killed the light. Facing her I listened to her breath as she drew closer.

Her lips touched mine then lingered as I felt a slight moan leave my lips and our mouths opened. She drew away, pecking me on the forehead.

"Not here. Not tonight," she said and turned over.

I pulled a deep breath and turned in the bed, letting my thoughts wander until I drifted off.

21

With the morning came a bright light stinging the back of my eyes. I pulled myself up in the bed with care to find Ally fast asleep with her mouth wide open and giving a view of her perfect molars. She stirred as I moved, her eyes peeking open and mouth closing to a grin.

"Morning," she said in a sleep-weary voice.

"Morning," I replied, mine not much different. "I'm heading back over. I can't face the family."

"I understand. I'll catch you later for a walk."

I nodded and bundled my insubstantial pile of clothes in my arms.

"Shit. My coat's back at the hotel."

"Open the wardrobe, borrow whatever you want. I won't watch," she said, and I caught a grin on her face as she turned the other way. "I'll drop your things off later."

Within a few minutes, in borrowed sweats, I was back at fifty-four. After a few moments more, I'd showered and changed into my own clothes, my things from the night before, including my underwear, in the wash before the house stirred. The white lace hung to dry in my room, not on display on the washing line outside with the other things I'd pegged out with the tiny dog nipping at my ankles.

Everyone in the house seemed in a good mood as they rose to the breakfast table I'd laid out, giving them a bonus as they hadn't expected me home so early. Despite Lenart's smile, he couldn't help but grill me about what happened last night and what had prompted my early return.

I told him very little, the time in the bar was the only part where I gave him any detail.

As I answered his questions, I couldn't help but think of what Ally had said; not only his questions about next door, I could understand those, but the suggestion of cameras in the room where I would often be naked. I gave a sudden shudder at the thought, but had to dismiss it. I needed to spend my day off figuring out how the hell I could properly use our next meeting, knowing I wouldn't have much time to prepare and wouldn't know the venue.

At least I knew it wouldn't be at the house and unlikely the same hotel. Could I use the promise of my virginity and the three of us playing together as a way of getting information about that room?

"Catarina," I heard Lenart say, rushing back from the place I'd drifted to in my mind; day dreaming was not something I would ever do.

"Sorry, I was in another world."

"Yes, I can see that," he said. I let his voice trail off again as he droned on about how I should clean the bathrooms a different way. When he finished speaking, I stood from the table and excused myself, watching as his face widened with alarm.

"What about the breakfast things?" he said, his voice building to a bluster.

"It's my day off," I said, my gaze catching the start of Celina's grin.

I spent the next few hours back in bed, dozing in and out of sleep, only half paying any attention to the hushed arguments between Celina and Lenart, punctuated with the occasional stomp of the children's feet up and down the stairs, followed by scrapes and clicks of the dog's excited chase.

The rest of my waking time I wracked my head with the challenge, coming up with ideas only to dash them moments later. One such idea surviving the first test was to break into the house, waiting until the right opportunity arose when both families were out.

The street was quiet most of the time; the other neighbours kept to themselves. But for the occasional car in the drives or lights behind curtains, I would guess they were unoccupied.

I hadn't seen an alarm on the building next door. Neither a box on the wall or a controller inside. I would have noticed. The thought mutated in my head as I lay on the pillow.

I could get hold of the keys, arrange a copy or just keep them and hope Frank didn't get the locks changed. If they had nothing to hide, then why would they go to the bother?

We'd trained to use moulding clay, or that blue sticky stuff, to grab the image of a key. I wasn't sure if they had the same thing in this place, or maybe they did and just used a different colour. If I had support I could give it to the local field lab or send it away in the post and receive it back by return. I had access to neither, no links, just the weekly messages on the computer and I was already late for my last report.

Would I need another meeting to get hold of the key?

Even if I had a key, I had to assume the place was being watched.

Rule one. Either outside or in, or both.

The plan drifted along and took a sharp turn. A disguise could work, although timing would be a problem. Fifty-six and fifty-four would have to be empty of all others, which wasn't impossible; in fact it happened quite a lot. My lot had family or other business which took them all away every so often. The others would go on trips, their details unknown.

I would have to travel out of the estate then come back wearing a disguise, with a new car. Getting the car wouldn't be a problem, just one of the many skills I'd picked up early in training. With tools from Lenart's shed I could get in and start an older car, but the black boxes and gadgets needed for the newer models were not available.

I could emerge all in black with a balaclava over my head. I'd park down the street and sneak down the fence line or appear from the woods less than a hundred footsteps to the front door, or hop over the fence line to the back. I'd soon find out if there was any surveillance. I would have to just deal with whatever I found.

Thoughts turned to the hotel. The guy with the gun. I tried to figure out if I'd explained myself well. It was a stupid mistake not to turn off my reactions, even though they were almost impossible to ignore and designed to stop me, or my charge, from dying.

A question popped into my head.

Would a multinational company want to have Frank dead? Or a government?

Of course I knew these things went on. I was, after all, one of the very instruments for the job, but if he was a legitimate businessman then he wouldn't be a target for our organisation. He would have to stray well off the moral path to become one, or be working against or with a foreign power to warrant a hit.

Or was I still naïve, despite all I knew?

I couldn't tell much about the hitman himself, other than he was slow and made a major mistake in standing so close to an unguarded door.

Waking from a deep sleep, I found the house quiet, the sound of the arguments gone, maybe just the TV on low in the front room.

Pulling out of bed, I felt refreshed and peeked out of my window and to the driveway.

One car gone. One still there. The bright light of the day still in full blaze.

I looked to next door and saw Frank coming out of his house. In the steep angle I could just make him out as he peered back along the lead at the dog who'd grown so much even in the last few weeks.

I watched as he shut the door, surveyed around before glancing in my direction, even though there was no chance he could have seen me behind the net curtain.

After pulling on my towelling robe, I opened my door to a crack at first to check there was no one there, then moved to the tall window in the hall, looking down the stair before getting a better view from the side window.

Who are you, Frank Bukia? I thought, watching as he led the dog between the houses.

Checking the time on my watch, I wondered why Ally hadn't joined him and why she hadn't called at the door.

Floating down the stairs with my feet to the edge of the

wood, a habit I'd already picked up even though there was no real need, I soon saw Lenart asleep in his chair with his hand still wrapped around a glass empty of the brown liquor he loved so much. He gave no movement as the dog jumped from his lap and bounded to me, knocking me sideways.

"Not yet," I whispered, despite knowing it would take much more to rouse the dirty old man from his drug-induced sleep.

The knock at the door wasn't enough either.

Ally.

A full ten minutes had passed since Frank had left the house and she grinned back at me as I answered the door, peering in to find the dog before shouting "Walkies" in a high tone.

The dog erupted in a frenzy of excitement, running to the cupboard and scratching at the door to get to his lead.

"We're going out then," I said, smiling back.

"I guess so," she replied with a lop-sided smile.

Humid air rolled through the doorway and handing over the leashed dog I ran upstairs to pull on a pair of shorts and a thin top to take in the rays.

Ally didn't stop talking, her words excited and in full swing, using her art of saying so much whilst giving little away. I didn't know what she was talking about. All I could get was she was about to explode if we didn't get somewhere soon so she could speak her mind. It must have been ten minutes of our fast pace before her words made sense.

"He's so made up about you. What you did," she said, flitting her head towards me then searching forward.

"It was just a reaction."

"I know, but you saved his life. Mine too," she said and without looking at me she linked her fingers into mine at my side.

"I think you were braver than me. You were standing in front of him," I said, squeezing her hand.

"A reaction too," she said, turning to me for a second.

"Do you love him?"

She paused and I heard movement to the side of the tree ahead.

"Girls," came a deep voice, a voice I'd expected. Frank.

Ally didn't answer my question, other than turning to face him with a broad grin.

"I thought we might meet you here," I said, looking at Ally, her broad mouth now a sideways smile.

"How are you?" he said, holding the dog's lead coiled in his hand. I let Fuzz off before he pulled my arm from its socket.

Distracted, I watched as he shot out into the undergrowth in a flurry of curly hair.

"A little delicate this morning," I replied.

"I heard you had your own little party. I hope you two girls behaved yourself together in that bed."

Ally nudged him with her elbow, giggling. "Of course we did."

"I don't know about you, but I had to go for a long run on the treadmill," he said, taking in a slow deep breath.

"I went back to bed," I said, and joined Ally's giggles, but stopped as I caught myself, straightening my lips and drawing a deep breath. I knew if I could see myself I'd be so ashamed.

"In all seriousness. I have a lot to thank you for, Cat, and your father, it would seem."

I smiled back.

"I was on autopilot. I don't really remember any of it."

"It was slick. Slicker than I've seen in many years. My boys are jealous, not that they'd admit it, and the way you ran into danger."

"Stupid, I know," I said, cutting him off.

"Not with those skills. We could use you."

"Frank," Ally butted in, her brow furrowed.

"What?" I replied.

"Don't worry," Frank said. "I'm just being silly."

Ally relaxed away from him and curled her arm around mine.

"So when are we…?" she said, looking back at Frank, but he cut her off before she could finish.

"Soon, but I better get back." He turned and called for the dog. "Ladies," he said with a short bow to each of us before heading the way we'd just come.

I felt a flutter of excitement as I watched him walk away.

22

After my Sunday chores the next day, I took the ball of fluff, the children and Celina on a hike into the woods, laden down with a picnic I'd prepared. I'd invited Lenart, but he'd scoffed at the idea; instead we left him sitting at the computer, tapping at the keys as he said something about a load of work he'd had dumped in his lap.

The children raced ahead on the path, running beside the dog as he darted this way and that to explore the undergrowth. It felt great to see them be like children should be, racing around rather than shut up in the house with their games and the TV.

I carried a wicker basket; Celina held a bag with two bottles of fizz and glasses she'd insisted were essential supplies for any adventure.

With the children out of sight, Celina's voice lowered. "Lenart worries about you," she said without turning towards me.

"Why?" I replied, not hiding my surprise.

"He thinks you're going off the rails."

"Off the rails?" I said, letting go of a snort of laughter. "Is my work suffering?"

"No, that's not what he means. Anyway, I told you, you do too much."

"So what does he mean?"

"Ever since the Bukia's moved back," she said, pausing, "he thinks you're spending too much time with Alarica."

"Does he now?"

"He thinks she's a bad influence."

"Oh," I replied, not sure how to respond. "What do you think?"

"I think you're very young, maybe too young to be away from your family."

"You employed me."

"And I'm glad we did, but I..." she paused for just a moment. "We want to make sure you're safe."

"From Alarica?"

"No. You know what I mean. Lenart thinks you're seeing someone. Seeing a man."

I let the pause hang without a reply, leaving our footsteps to punctuate each empty second that went past.

"I want you to enjoy yourself. I said it to you before. You're too young to be stuck inside. You have the rest of your life to tie yourself to a house. The sink. The children. Have fun, but just be careful."

The silence hung between us as we walked, both of us listening to the excited voices of the children in the distance, their cries of play getting closer.

"And I'm really sorry for what I nearly did."

"Don't be silly," I said.

"No, I am," she replied, looking down to the ground. "I was nearly the one you had to be wary of. The one who tried to take advantage."

I linked my arm into hers and pulled up close to her, hugging her arm as we walked.

"Don't be silly. What's the worst that could have happened? Anyway, it would have been fun. You were just trying to give me one of those new experiences you keep talking about."

She turned and smiled, hugging my arm in return.

"Don't you start," she said, sucking air in through her teeth.

By now the sound of the children's voices had changed, the excitement hushed. They were still talking, but were off the path, their sounds coming from an area dense with trees. We unlinked our arms and took high steps to climb over the undergrowth and tall ferns, navigating through the trunks.

A minute in we could see the children in a clearing, light breaking through the small gap in the canopy above. The children were standing over a raised, wide, circular concrete structure rising to the boy's knee. With the dog wagging its tail at their feet, they peered inside with wide eyes.

With one hand on the rust-stained concrete, the boy

hovered over the opening, which was wide enough for a person to squeeze into. A small stone dropped through the open top of the pipe and soon hit the bottom with a dull thud.

"Jimmy," Celina snapped. Both the children and the dog turned, shocked expressions glaring back toward us.

"Look, Celina," he said, pointing down to the pipe.

As we stepped forward, we could see the pipe was a little bigger than a car tyre and open ended, but just below the edge of the opening sat a rusted grill, each of the bars more than twice the thickness of one of my fingers. To the side furthest away a large, dulled chrome padlock clamped it shut. Taking a step forward, I peered down into darkness.

"It's a drain," Celina said as she backed away.

I looked on. Although dark inside, I could just about see to the dry bottom, its base full of decayed leaves moving around as if teeming with life.

"And the perfect place for lunch."

The children cheered, turning their attention away and to the hamper as we unloaded the contents across the blanket.

23

Three days later, the next parcel arrived. On hearing the bell, Celina opened the door to find the box, smaller than the last, on the mat, only giving a quiet announcement across the house.

Busying myself wrist deep in the dishwater, I waited until she left for the tennis club, which since our talk she seemed to have resigned herself to attending on her regular schedule. After the washing up, I did a few more jobs, clearing away my tasks for the day as I tried to stifle the unwanted anticipation.

I tried to forget it was there. I tried to let myself get on with the day, but passing by the shallow hall table I picked the box up, feeling as if an electrical charge ran up my hand as I touched the pale cream cardboard wrapped with ribbon and my name written on the front in the same hand.

I tried to hold back thoughts of what could be within the package which felt so much lighter than the last one. Pushing it away inside my top dresser drawer, I left the room, pulled the door closed and drew a deep breath. After a pause, rather than heading down the stairs, I turned back, stepped into my room and pulled the door closed behind me.

I lingered with my hand hovering over the drawer handle and turned, staring at the full-length mirror. For a moment I didn't recognise myself.

"Pull yourself together," I said to my reflection.

Sitting on the bed, I laid the box on my lap, my fingers plucking at the delicate ribbon. Closing my eyes, I drew the box to my nose and took a long draw of the scent I remembered from that last night.

Letting it back down to my lap, I lifted the lid and the first flap of tissue paper, taking the beautiful handwritten note.

My Dear Cat,

I'm so excited we'll finally do this. A car will pick you up from your house around 4pm on Saturday. Bring the same as before and wear the same style, you got it spot on.

So sorry for the shaky hand, I'm bristling with excitement at the memory as I write. The driver will drop you off the next day. Everything will go to plan this time, we've made sure. In the box is a thank you from our friend. You know why.

Wear it and you can leave it on, or take it off with the rest of your things, if you like!

Excitedly,
A xx xx xx

Underneath the note lay a simple golden chain. Letting the delicate links run through my fingers, I pulled it from its paper bed to find a shining charm the size and shape of a small almond dangling narrow end up. An intricate pattern of twists and turns ran across the silvered surface.

Examining the detail, I found a tiny hinge on the top edge by the loop connecting it to the chain. Squeezing the sides and with a tiny snap of an unseen clasp, it leafed open at the top to reveal a diamond the size of a pea.

Sucking on my bottom lip I watched, wide-eyed, as the stone sparkled so bright in the light through the window, marvelling as the shell formed delicate wings of a beautiful creature, its body the shimmering diamond.

"A hidden gem," I said out loud, my smile stretching out my cheeks.

Standing, I clasped the jewel around my neck, my head light as I marvelled at its reflection.

My first ever gift from an admirer, the symbol not lost on me.

The waiting was worse than before. At least last time I'd thought we were supposed to be only next door, the change of venue thrust upon me, so I didn't need to worry. This time I had no clue, but still I couldn't help thinking of the possibilities.

I thought of finding Ally. I thought of quizzing her on where we would go, but I knew that like last time she was holding herself back and wouldn't tell me even if I could get to speak with her. Instead, I tried to focus on my own objectives; those of the assignment.

My last plan had been to get them impaired through drink and maybe a few tablets, then talk and find out what it was all about, hoping they'd let something slip. Maybe even for them to bring me into their trust and get a tour, or find my own means of entry. Now I knew some of those would never happen, no matter how far I went with letting them do whatever they had planned.

I shook away distracting thoughts and I tried to

concentrate on objectives.

Get them talking.

Find out why the hell I could be here.

Get a key. Either the front or back door would do. The rest I'd figure out when I could.

Try not to lose my virginity to someone I hardly knew and to someone who was becoming a good friend. Or maybe not just a friend.

But what would be the worst thing if I did it? If I went through with the deed?

Their guard would come down at the very least. I couldn't help imagining how the night would go.

I would arrive and we would have drinks at a bar or some hotel suite. He'd meet me downstairs and talk, not heading up to the bedroom straight away.

The place might be public, but I guessed that wouldn't be the case from Ally's letter. They'd taken care to make sure we weren't disturbed this time.

I'd drink too much. I already knew that, to help with the nerves, balancing on the line of control. We'd stay away from the bedroom longer than Ally would like. I wondered what she was more eager for; me and her or watching me and him. Maybe there would be no distinction.

My heart raced at both thoughts, but each for different reasons.

Frank would want to stay and drink for a while, to talk, to build up his appetite; that's what he'd said. But barring any raids on the building, we'd head up the stairs. They would lead me into a big bedroom with a wide bed; an emperor or bigger, if such a thing existed.

We would kiss. We'd undress. Who would first, I wasn't sure, or perhaps at the same time?

We'd take our time. I would have to linger in my bra and knickers, or else why had they gone to the trouble? He would want to see me, what he could spy just underneath. He'd hold himself back for as long as he dared.

I wondered what he'd instructed Ally to wear. Would

we be twins? Or was the white just for me, this once only?

We would kiss again. One on one, or all three. Me and Ally first, putting on a show. Building the tension. The pressure rising for everyone.

Hands would be everywhere, all over, mouths too. All this would be new to me. My senses overwhelmed with new sights. New smells. New tastes.

Then it would happen. They would lay me down and in it would go. It would be quick, maybe with a little pain, but it would soon be over. The build-up would see to that. For me and for him, no doubt.

We'd recover and he would have to take his turn on Ally. I'd watch. I would enjoy that, too. And then that would be it, or maybe once or twice more.

We would sleep, then start again in the morning, but that would be it. When we were back, maybe he'd call. Maybe I would get an invitation, another hand delivered box? Perhaps he would move on.

I didn't know if that could be true. Of course I could ask. What would I do if that was it? Deflower me and move on.

But to me it's not a real thing. It's only important in my head, I suppose, and to him and to other men, but I don't care about that.

Do I?

Anyway, the aim was not to do those things. Wasn't it?

I could just get blind drunk. They could still have me, but I doubt they would.

I don't think.

I'm not sure Ally would let him rape my unconscious body. If he did, maybe she would have no choice, then I would lose it and not have known; not have the experience I guess would be the payment for it going.

Of course there is my professionalism. I was working. Set a task, although not an objective. In training we never dealt with how we should react. How professional was it to sleep with a target?

113

Not that he was officially anything.

I'd been told to watch their house, not the person. And anyway, who would know apart from me? And, of course, Ally.

Maybe Dr Devlin if I wrote it here.

Ally would watch, involved too. I'd have sex with them both. The same issue twice over, I guessed.

I didn't know.

I didn't know if I wanted my first guy to be anyone, let alone someone linked to my work, someone who I may have to target later down the line; to detain or otherwise take action against. Or kill.

I didn't know if I wanted my first girl to be in this way. Ally was turning in to as good a friend as I'd ever found, better perhaps. No. Much better.

I paused, checking the word fit. Friend was not quite right, not enough for what I thought, but I didn't dare think about what suited more.

Celina was not far from the mark either, but she had issues and I didn't think it would do either of us any good. It could of course be her making.

I wasn't sure of anything. What did any of it matter?

After all the thoughts racing around in my head, I made my mind up not to decide until I was there. I would fly by the seat of my pants, like I'd had to so many times before.

I knew the arguments for and against and I'd have to do what I was good at; get in a state of mind and react to whatever took place. I could always say I'd changed my mind, or maybe I would get a headache.

I could watch and see how it went down. What went where.

I'd had enough of my thoughts and hiding the gift away; I ran for over an hour. It was that or break out the stubby toy. But not in this house, not at the thought of Lenart's cameras.

Venting my frustration on my feet, I used the energy to improve my time, and it was getting dark as I arrived back to

Celina with the kids. She'd already put the dinner on and beamed back at me as I came through the front door.

Lenart stood by the fireplace, his face bunched with anger.

"Is it from a boyfriend?" he said, catching me in the kitchen with no one else around.

I stood still, shocked at his attack.

"You can't afford these sorts of distractions," he said, edging forward.

That was it. I had no idea why the hell he thought he had any power over me. I almost felt like fucking Frank just to piss off this stupid old man.

Taking a deep breath, I caught my thoughts before they could morph into action. I was not a teenager. Not a child. I was a professional young lady in pursuit of a very important career. This guy in front of me was irrelevant.

"If you want me to leave I will," I replied.

"What makes you say that?" he said, his face widening in surprise.

"I'm not a child. Not your child. I do my work and I fulfil my end of the contract you pay me for. That is how it works. There is nothing else, will be nothing else. Get used to that or I'll leave. You cannot treat me like this," I replied. I'd had enough of his shit.

He turned and for the first time saw Celina in the doorway. I hadn't seen her there, either.

"She's right, you know," she said. "She's the hired help. I'm not sure what else you could want for, but she gives us everything she's meant to. The rest of the time she should get on with her life. That's what's meant to happen. It's what I should have done."

Lenart stood facing her, his body unmoving. He turned around and glanced in my direction. I swear if I'd been smiling he would have swung at me and then at her. But no, I didn't smile because I knew how much it had taken Celina to say those things and I knew she would have to pay some price for the words.

He stormed off, snatching open the drinks cabinet door then banged up the stairs before slamming the bedroom door.

"Thank you," I said.

"I wouldn't thank me. It was as much for me as it was for you."

"Thank you anyway," I said, wrapping my arms around her.

"I think this might come to an end soon."

"My job?" I replied in a flat tone.

"Mine, too," she said, nodding. "Our relationship, I mean. I've had enough."

I kissed her on the cheek and went up to my room.

24

Saturday came too soon again, and I hadn't seen Ally since receiving the gift. I couldn't decide if I thought she was just busy or saving herself for this evening.

Since Lenart confronted me, I'd spent more time in my room than I had since I'd arrived at the house. He'd stopped drinking the laced whiskey and would instead follow Celina around, hounding her, always getting at her for little things as if taking out his frustrations on her because he couldn't get to me.

Celina had said she thought my time was ending and I thought she might be right. At this address at least. I couldn't help but wonder if the news would elicit more than the standard response. *Observe. Report.*

I would have to do this all from another base.

Pushing those thoughts out of my mind, I ignored the detail of Lenart's grumbles as I drove his car off the driveway, Celina's still not working since I loosened one of the engine's HT leads.

I busied myself with the stroll around the supermarket, then after unloading the bags I concentrated the rest of my day on preparations.

In the bath I kept myself covered under the bubbles as much as I could, then stood in front of my bedroom mirror in just the lacy whites, wrapping the chain around my neck with the unsheathed diamond hanging in the light.

Staring at my image I took a deep breath, eventually pushing the diamond home and pulling on the second batch of thin clothes which only went some way to covering me up.

I waited until I saw the car pull outside, a black Mercedes, its paintwork so polished I could see myself even from my room.

Pulling on my long coat, I shot down the stairs and out of the door, calling back at the last minute that I would see everyone tomorrow as the door closed.

Searching Alarica out in the dark interior, I was a little

surprised to find no one other than the driver behind the blacked-out windows as I opened the door before he had a chance to do it for me. The middle-aged man greeted me with a nod of his cap and pointed out the fridge, asking if I would like him to open the champagne.

I told him I could manage and uncorked the bottle. There was no chance I was going to wherever it was without having had something to drink.

With my glass charged I leant forward and asked where we were going, but as I'd suspected, the destination would remain a surprise and I should relax and enjoy the ride.

We drove for an hour and with the bottle empty, the car pulled off the wide high-speed road, the flat land beginning to undulate and line with a dense covering of trees either side.

Another half an hour passed and I declined another bottle just before the car slowed. Still I couldn't see much other than the trees.

"Where are we?" I said as the car stopped.

"We're in the middle of nowhere," he replied and pulled himself out of the car, soon opening my door to give me the first proper look at what appeared to be a two-storey log cabin.

No public.

No other guests.

The realisation hit. Here he could do what he wanted with little or no chance of interruption.

The wide front door opened and the driver wished me all the best as he left my side to hand over my bag to a tall man in a morning suit.

"Good evening, ma'am," the old gent said in a stiff English accent, his hand waving me inside.

"Thank you," I replied and watched the glimmer of recognition of my accent in his eyes. "Are the others here?" I said, walking over the threshold.

"Yes. They are in the pool house," he replied.

"The pool house?" I mouthed.

"Can I take your coat?"

I shook off my coat and watched as he slid a few steps to the side, pulling open a cupboard door and disappearing my coat under the dark wooden stairs rolling to the floor above.

"If you would like to follow me," he said, seeming unfazed by the amount of skin I had on show.

Keeping quiet, I followed through door after door, winding our way across the house, passing orange glowing lamps hanging down from dark wooden-panelled walls.

Soon we arrived at a white plastic door out of keeping with the rest of what I'd seen, but the chlorine in the air as it opened betrayed its reason.

Holding open the door, the butler stood to the side and ushered me forward, not following as I took slow steps from the carpet to the light tiled floor with my gaze fixed on the Olympic-sized pool as voices chatted in the distance.

With the door closing at my back I saw Frank laying on a lounger in just a pair of bright-blue speedos. Ally sat up on another to his side with a book held out in front of her. She wore a tiny red bikini and let the book drop, her eyes widening as she saw me.

Ally frantically waved as Frank looked at me down his nose before he sat up to pull on a towelling robe. At first I couldn't quite put my finger on their matching expression, but as I walked towards them I realised they looked like it was their birthday and I was the cake.

Ally stood, strutting along the side of the pool, leaving the robe behind and letting me take in her full view as she walked towards me.

After taking me in her arms, hugging tight, she finally released and led me towards where Frank stood uncorking the champagne, his face fixed with a wide grin.

"What is this place?" I said, looking around the pool. I gazed at the wall of glass which ran the complete length of the room, focusing on a lake which sprawled out to the horizon.

"Ours for the night," Ally replied, jumping on the spot.

"Just somewhere I get the use of. A perk of the job."

"Frank," Ally said, laughing, pushing her hand out to rub his towelling-covered chest.

"I didn't bring a suit?" I said.

Ally laughed as her eyebrows raised.

"I didn't want to ruin the surprise, but I have spares. Or there are other alternatives," she said, giving a playful tug at the bow holding the cups of her bikini top tight to her skin.

"I bet you could do with a drink," Frank said, staring at Ally's chest as she stopped short of letting the bow slip.

He didn't wait for me to answer and turned, filling glasses arranged on a long table near where they'd been laying. "Give me five minutes," he said, handing over a glass. "Have a look around and I'll be back in something a little more decent."

An odd choice of words, I thought. "And you too, Al," he said to his side.

"Yes, of course," she replied with a smile filling the left side of her mouth. "Five minutes, maybe ten," she added, still giggling.

Walking away, they disappeared through a door to the back of the long room at the opposite end to where the butler had shown me in. They would be much longer, I was sure.

Sipping at the champagne, I stared out across the lake with its glass-like surface disturbed by only the occasional ripple. Turning, I took small steps back the way I'd come, heading through the door and past the endless panelling to cast my gaze over the various pictures, each some anonymous landscape or ancient portrait. There were no photos. Nothing personal to him.

This place had corporate written all over it.

I found my way back to the entrance hall and crossed over, peering in each of the rooms on the ground floor. I found a drawing room with comfy over-stuffed leather chairs, a wall filled with liquor bottles, the air heavy with long-stale cigar smoke. It was an old man's room, or a man's man room, the place where all the guys would go after a meal in days gone by. They may as well put a sticker on the door; No Women Allowed.

Finding the dining room next door, a long table stood set for three places, one at each end and another in the middle. I figured it could seat twenty or more with plenty of room for elbows.

The next room had a more modern feel, with two large couches centred around a thirty-something-inch TV on a deep unit set up against a long wall. I heard the stairs creak and nipped into the bathroom to take a minute.

As I came out, Ally followed Frank from the floor above. She wore the same as she had the last time, except for a different shade of top; a deep red. Frank wore dark trousers and a short sleeved white shirt, thin enough to make out a dark matt of hair covering his chest.

"Sorry for the delay," he said, despite being back well within ten minutes. "What do you think of the place?"

"It's amazing," I replied.

"Isn't it? And in the middle of nowhere so there's no chance anyone can disturb us. I've sent Jeeves off for the night, so we'll have to fend for ourselves, but we get our privacy. I hope that's all right?"

"He's not called that," I said, unable to control my laughter.

"He is," Frank replied with a wide smile. Ally nodded at his side, her face lit. "You all right with looking after ourselves?"

"I'm used to doing things for myself."

Ally burst out laughing. "Not for want of offers," she said, looking me up and down.

"Very good," I replied.

"Shall we eat?" Frank asked. "You girls go sit down and I'll grab the trolley from the kitchen."

Ally came down the final steps while Frank disappeared along the corridor. She took me by the hand and led me back into the dining room.

"You're wearing everything like last time?" she asked

as she led me down the long table.

"And the necklace," I replied with a grin and Ally stopped, turning toward me. Reaching to my neck, she pinched the silver and opened its wings.

"It's beautiful, isn't it," she said, staring down at the gem I knew would be gleaming.

"It is," I replied. "You chose it, didn't you?"

She turned and caught me staring, then nodded before leaning forward to plant a soft kiss on my lips.

"You get to sit in the middle," she said, turning around with a brisk swirl.

"Like I'm on display?"

"Yes, because you are. Now sit."

25

Doing as I'd been told, I settled in the seat, resting my glass on the coaster in front of me. In the background I could hear the roll of trolley wheels growing louder as they rattled along the wooden floor. The trolley arrived moments later, with Frank's features set with concentration as he manoeuvred it around the table.

Looking up, he beamed back at us on seeing we both sat in the seats he'd expected and were watching his arrival. In turn, he placed a cloche-covered plate at each setting, starting with mine, then came back, topping up each glass, before one by one revealing the lobster salad laid out with such care as he took away the metal covers.

I dug into the food with an appetite I hadn't realised had developed, grateful for the distraction from talking. Instead, I listened to their chat, which in most part was benign, but as I took the last mouthful, I felt their focus back in my direction.

"So, Catarina," Frank said, "tell me about yourself. All I know is what Al's been telling me."

"Well, you know how beautiful she is," Ally said, raising her glass before I could say anything. Frank nodded and tipped his glass in my direction as he waited for me to speak.

I took a deep breath, trying to slow the warmth building in my cheeks.

"There's not much to tell."

"Don't be shy," Ally said. "We want to get to know you. We want to know you inside and out."

I smiled back and took a long drink, stifling a sneeze as the bubbles hit the back of my throat.

"I was born in the UK and raised all over the place. My dad was in the Air Force," I said, as was my normal explanation.

Frank raised his eyebrows as I spoke.

"We eventually settled in a town in Sussex. After school, I went off to university and studied languages. It gave me an opportunity to take some time out and to travel, so I took it and here I am."

"And you came here? Of your own free will?" Frank said with a wide smile, his brow a little furrowed. "We speak English, too?"

"Barely," Ally chipped in, not able to stop herself laughing. Frank glanced over at her before turning back to me.

"It's stop number one," I said.

Frank raised his eyebrows and I couldn't mistake Ally's sharp intake of breath.

"Since when?" she said.

"Since for always," I replied, turning to see her wide-eyed concern. "I'm not going yet. But I do think I'm outstaying my welcome with the Rozman's."

"Hah," Ally snorted.

"Al," Frank snapped. "Be nice. You don't really know them." He turned back to me. "So how long do you think you'll stay?"

"Well, if the Rozman's want me gone, then I might take the opportunity, but I'd like to hang around for a few more weeks at least."

He nodded, saying nothing.

"What about you, Ally?" I asked, turning towards her.

Ally smiled and looked from me to Frank. "I'll stay as long as I'm needed," she said, her voice sounding soft and dreamy.

Frank gave a light cough into his napkin and stood to take the champagne and walked around the table to fill each of our glasses.

"Tell her," she said as he sat back down and I watched as he glared at her for a moment.

"Before you decide, come and talk to me," he said. "There's dessert if you want it?" he added before I could ask any more.

"We're counting on it," Ally replied with a giggle and I turned to see her looking me up and down with her head tilted to the side. "Let's go somewhere more comfortable," she said, standing with her glass.

My heart rate spiked. I wasn't ready. I was nowhere near ready.

I hadn't had a chance to form a plan. If I was being honest, for a moment I hadn't even been thinking about the mission I'd given myself.

Still I stood, following Ally and Frank, relieved when we passed by the bottom of the stairs and headed into the living room where I'd seen the sofas and the big TV.

Frank took a couch; I took the other. Ally looked between us, raising her eyebrows, but eventually she sat next to me even though there were another two spaces available. Frank's smile wasn't his only sign she'd made the right choice.

She rested her back against my upper body and with the top of her shoulder warm against my skin, I tried not to look too uncomfortable as Frank's smile beamed from the opposite end of the room.

"So what about your upbringing?" he said, fidgeting in his seat.

"Sheltered, as you can imagine. We were a close community, even though we moved every three years. The place was safe. It was one of the last places you could leave your doors unlocked at night."

"Did you ever have a boyfriend?" Ally asked. As she spoke she kicked off her heels before swinging her feet onto the chair and lowering herself down my front so the back of her head rested just above my left breast.

"No. I wasn't interested," I replied with the truth.

"A girlfriend?" she said slowly, and I watched the corner of Frank's mouth turn up.

"No," I said, again without lying.

"Have you ever had a kiss?" Ally asked, with Frank's gaze locked to her face as his grin grew.

"Of course. I'm not a nun," I said, a little louder than I'd meant to.

"Girl or boy?" Frank said, surprising me.

"Both," I replied.

"But not at the same time?" he said, his voice flat as if put on.

"Not yet." I knew it was the answer he was looking for, his wide smile confirming.

"And you're a virgin," he said, his tone making it clear it wasn't a question.

"Yes," I replied anyway. "Enough about me. Ally, tell me about you," I said, my hand stroking her upper arm. "When did you lose your virginity?"

"How do you know I'm not…"

I laughed, and she stopped protesting.

"You've told me all the details in Technicolor," I replied.

"Have you now?" Frank said, with a sideways look at her, the wide questioning grin bunching his cheeks.

"I was eighteen," she replied. "A fumble in the dark, over in seconds. Way too messy for my liking."

"A boy then?" I raised my eyebrows as I spoke.

"Of course. With a woman it lasts so much longer. No one's in a rush to get to the end."

"Don't mind me," Frank said, pretending to be offended.

"Most men," Ally added, tilting her head up to take a drink.

"And with a woman?" I said when she'd placed the glass back to the carpet.

"A year later. It was just a bit of fun to pass the time. I could never be serious with a woman, but I love fooling around."

"Maybe you haven't met the right woman," Frank said to my surprise.

"Or maybe I have," Ally blurted, rubbing her head into my chest so the back of her neck, intentionally or otherwise, sent a flurry of sensation through the tip of my nipple.

"So what about you, Frank?" I replied, emptying my glass.

"About fifteen, summer camp," came his deep voice.

"Man or woman?" I asked with a smirk.

"Woman. Girl. She was the same age."

"So have you ever kissed a man?" Ally added.

"No," he replied, letting his shoulders stiffen.

"So you're a virgin, too," I said. Ally and I laughed out loud.

Frank let the laughter die and stood.

"I'll get another bottle," he said, but I shuffled forward and Ally moved.

"I'll get it. I need the bathroom anyway."

"Okay," he replied. "The kitchen's on the right and you'll find the bottles in the left-hand fridge."

I stood, feeling a little unsteady on my feet. I slipped off the heels and left them by the door. Frank stood as I went through, but didn't follow me out.

I faced the under-stairs cupboard, pausing for only a moment before I pulled open the door and found my coat where the butler had placed it. Pushing my hand into the inner pocket, I found the small bag of pills still in place.

As their laughter poured from the room I'd just left, I let the door close and headed the few paces to the bathroom. Sitting on top of the toilet with the lid down and being careful not to pierce the bag, I crushed up the pills between my fingers. The result was a powder not as fine as I'd achieved with the mortar and pestle at the Rozman's, but it would have to do.

Hiding the bag in the left cup of my bra, I looked in the mirror. The material was so delicate and thin, the top so tight I could see the outline of the bag and the lump of pills making me look deformed. I tried holding the bag in the waistband of my skirt, but it dropped out too easily the moment I moved.

For a moment I thought about hiding them down my underwear but I still didn't know if I'd be wearing them for much longer.

Drawing a deep breath, I tried to steady my excitement. I tried to ignore the rush of energy through my body every time my skin touched Ally's.

I had to hold out. I had a purpose. I had to get hold of the keys.

I tried to focus.

I tried to remember back to the cupboard where I'd seen Ally's coat, but the rest of the cupboard was bare.

Now I'd spent too much time in the toilet and knew they would wonder if I was okay.

Compressing the bag into my fist, I opened the door whilst listening out. Hearing Ally's playful laughter, I headed to the kitchen.

What I found was the most modern room I'd seen so far, with granite worktops, white-tiled walls and two large fridges standing side by side. The left fridge was full to bursting with champagne. All different brands.

I pulled one from the top of the stack and popped the cork with care, capturing it in my hand. Listening out, I let the vapour draw away. With the laughter still distant, a sudden thought came to me.

What if they had already started getting frisky, taking the chance while I was out? Would I arrive back to their bodies naked and writhing on the floor?

I stopped the thought dead. I couldn't think like that. I had to react to whatever situation I found.

Pulling open the baggy, I tried to work the last lumps smaller against the work surface with the base of the bottle, stopping as I realised a tiny split had formed as a thin white powder covered the surface. I carefully pulled up the bag and let a small amount of the contents flow into the bottle.

Pausing, I peered through the dark glass, watching as the bubbles attached to the lumpy powder, taking the slow journey to settle to the bottom. I poured more in, a large amount this time and bubbles rolled to the top of the bottle, but subsided before spilling out.

I poured the remainder in and as I watched the bubbles settle, I heard a deep voice from the doorway.

26

"Are you okay?"

I turned away from the bottle to see Frank leaning on the door frame and peering toward me with a raised eyebrow.

"You gave me a fright," I replied, clutching the thin bag tight into my fist resting on the counter, hoping he couldn't see it.

"Is there a problem?" he said.

"No, just taking a moment to build up courage," I said, drawing a pronounced breath as I picked up the cork in the same hand as the bag.

"Don't be silly, there's nothing to be worried about. We'll take our time, enjoy ourselves and if tonight isn't the night and you're not ready, there's no pressure."

I listened, surprised at the sweetness of his words, already feeling myself relax in his presence.

"Come back in," he said, beckoning me through the kitchen door.

Heading towards him I glanced down at the base of the bottle, my look fixing on the tiny particles I could make out way too easily, but just as I looked up in hope Frank hadn't followed my look, I saw a wooden bowl on the worktop and a set of keys sitting in the centre. His Mercedes key sat pronounced on the pile. As he held the door open, I dropped the cork and the baggy through the lid of the bin as I passed.

Following Frank back into the lounge, I was more than a little surprised to see Ally still sitting in the same place and fully clothed as she inspected her nails with a dreamy expression.

As we came through the door, her face lit up. My chest tightened and my heart raced; in the moment I couldn't tell if it was the thrill of the operation or Ally's short skirt riding up that caused my beat to pound. I scarcely noticed as Frank took the bottle, topping up each flute as I retook my seat. Ally's head came back to rest at my chest, this time a little lower, but still with the same electrifying effect.

We were soon back in conversation again, the pair sipping at the drinks whilst I was mindful to take the bare minimum. We spoke about the house, with Frank never revealing its true location despite my gentle probing.

He told me of the seven bedrooms, offering a tour a little later on. As predictable as clockwork, Ally joked they'd only be needing one tonight, and not for sleeping.

Asking about his work, he seemed more than happy to answer. He told about the company, an outsourced research partner to a major pharmaceutical. They were concentrating on specialist areas of interest, but the conversation dropped as Ally jumped up, sending a sudden shockwave through my chest as she pronounced we should cut the chat and play a game.

A sudden dread came over me at the thought of what she might suggest.

"Hide and seek," I blurted out.

Ally replied with a scathing look, much to Frank's amusement.

"A game to get us closer, not further apart."

Shrugging, I knew what her first suggestion would be just as she spoke. "Spin the bottle."

"Don't be too eager," Frank replied, shutting her down with a hand in the air, just as she spoke again.

"Twister," she said, the words turning to a high giggle.

"How about truth or dare?" I said.

Frank's eyebrows raised, but Ally said the words I'm sure he thought.

"But you're as pure as the driven snow. Surely you have nothing interesting to hide. If you do, just tell us," she said, raising her eyebrows.

"Okay, not truth or dare."

"Hey, ladies, I'm not a student anymore. Why don't we show Catarina the view from the pool house? It'll be dark soon."

I saw Ally deflate as I jumped at the chance.

"I'd love to," I said, raising up.

We stood and I followed Frank with Ally at my back.

"I'll meet you there," she said and veered off towards the bathroom.

As we headed through the second door, Frank spoke. "I'm sorry about Al."

"Don't be, it's fine," I said, shaking my head as he flashed a look toward me then carried on the journey.

"She's a little overexcited I think and maybe more than a little frustrated about last time," he replied, bunching up his cheeks as he twisted back to show his smile.

"I can imagine."

"But I don't think she understands that you might be nervous and not want to jump into bed as soon as you arrive," he said, stopping to open the plastic of the pool house door.

About to reply, the words didn't come when I saw the sky darkening from blue to a deep grey through the long wall of windows. An orange sun lit up half the horizon and reflected its beauty across the mirror-still water.

"It's beautiful," I said, the words barely coming out.

"It is," he replied in a soft voice.

I turned towards him and he turned to me. Our eyes locked as he stooped and I raised up to my toes. As our lips touched, his moustache wafted across my nose. It felt as if I drew off his energy, a current working its way through my body to touch every part of my skin with a tiny crackle of electricity.

We held there for what seemed like hours, our lips not moving, pulling apart only as the door opened at our side. I drew back, fearful of her reaction.

"Now that's better," she said, her hands pushing out three full flutes. "Drink up," she said, flashing her eyebrows toward me. "He's a good kisser, isn't he?"

I nodded with a slight bow of my head as I took a gulp of the drink before I remembered what I'd put in the glass.

Before long we took a slow walk back to the lounge, Frank and Ally drinking like it was going out of season whilst I emptied my glass at every point I could; a plant pot here, a bin there.

Arriving back, Ally made a point of topping the drinks up. Looking at the near-empty bottle I saw the thin line of crystals had settled to the bottom as bubbles streamed upward as fast as ever.

I sat, but Ally didn't, instead walking over to Frank to plant a deep kiss on his lips. Not a sensual touch or a subtle peck, she landed a smacker of a mouth-shaker as if she was feeding on his face. Both took deep breaths when she eventually pulled back so I could see their lips red and bloated.

Ally turned toward me and I knew what would come next. I pushed myself back into the seat, barely hearing Frank's words as I stared at the wide grin walking towards me.

"Al. Be gentle."

Ally turned back to him with a devil's expression, one eyebrow raised and a wide grin pulling at the same side of her face. She turned back, her head bearing in toward me as she lowered, her lips soon plunging onto mine with a gentle touch that took me by surprise.

She kept still at first then slowly increased the pressure, moving her mouth. From nowhere and without thought, I replied with my own force, then my tongue, feeling her surprise at its touch, soon matching the dance with her own.

In the moment I could have been anywhere. In the moment I had no cares in the world, everything forgotten. Kissing Ally felt the most natural feeling in the world; so much different to Frank only moments earlier.

The world came into focus as she drew back, but only my surroundings. For a moment, as I regained my breath, I forgot all about who I really was. This was everything. In this room and standing in front of me was Ally and her wide, eager smile.

"Don't worry. She gives as good as she gets," Ally said, turning to Frank and both of us giggling at the tent in his trousers.

The kiss. Frank's words. Maybe the alcohol. Maybe the drugs. Any one of those could have decided; it was time to lose what I hadn't been trying to keep.

Standing with a great confidence, I watched Ally knock back her drink, her eyes lighting as she clearly liked what she saw in my expression.

Handing the empty glass to Frank who looked on, his eyes wide as if about to burst, I pulled her face towards mine and drove my tongue into her mouth.

She responded in kind, pulling me towards her by my shoulders, our chests touching, both of us releasing a moan of pleasure. As we kissed, her hands ran down my back, stopping as they reached the arch to pull up my top. I pulled away from her lips, raising my hands into the air and she had my top off within a breath, throwing it for Frank to catch.

Our lips met once again and Ally turned me to the side, pulling back for a moment to beam towards Frank. I didn't glance in his direction, instead kept my attention on her lips until she turned back to find me again.

It was my turn and with my hands at her back, I grabbed her top and pulled it free as we parted. I didn't stop there; instead my fingers found the clasp of her crimson bra, just like mine in every other way and she eagerly let her arms up to be freed, swinging the discards in Frank's direction.

I pushed my face back to hers, my hands touching at the softness of her breasts at what seemed like a furious pace, pinching her nipples between my fingers. My bra had gone before I'd realised her fingers and thumb were tugging at the end of my stiff nipples.

I bent, sucking hers into my mouth, slowing and taking my time with each as her head threw back with sharp breaths synchronised with the rise and fall of her chest. She held the back of my head tight, pressing further until I pulled up and she bent, her mouth taking its turn on mine.

I let out a deep moan as her finger brushed between my legs; my muschi, letting out a rush of laughter, a shower of sparks flying up my body.

She stood and backed herself up, licking drips from her finger as if it were an ice cream.

"She's fucking soaking wet," she said, her voice breathy.

I didn't move to see Frank's face, but I imagined him holding himself, stiff in his hands, unable to do anything but stroke. The thoughts vanished as in one move she turned me on the spot and she pushed me back, dropping me to the sofa. I closed my eyes as she pulled my legs into the air, tugging my knickers past my feet and spreading me wide before burying her head between.

Her tongue danced and too soon I burst in an explosion as I forced her head deeper into my crotch, screaming out as waves of joy kept washing over.

I took a deep breath and watched Ally's head bob up as she lowered my legs, her wide grin soaked.

I smiled back, a little coy as I took in the warm glow embracing my body, bucking at every tiny movement of her hand between my legs.

A strange breathy noise turned us both in Frank's direction.

He was asleep with his head tilted to the side, the zip of his trouser open, but whatever lived there had crawled back inside. In his hand were my knickers, the crotch still damp, the rest of our clothes spread around him. Ally turned back, at first wide-eyed, then gave a huge yawn and I replied with my own.

"That wasn't quite the reaction I was expecting," I said to Ally with a furrowed brow.

"It might have been my fault," she replied, wiping her face with her hand before licking at her fingers. "I thought we might need to liven up, so I put a little something in the champagne. I guess I got the wrong ones," she said, pulling a great yawn again. "I think we need to get him to bed."

"But it's your turn," I replied, trying not to smirk too much.

She paused, but only for a moment, lingering on his sorry sight before she took my hand, leading me up the stairs and to the bedroom.

Within another half an hour, we were both spent twice over and fell asleep in each other's arms.

When I woke the lamp was still on at the side of the bed and it was dark beyond the curtains.

With my head throbbing and mouth baked, I licked at my dry lips and memories flooded back, as did the picture of the fruit bowl in the kitchen.

Pulling up with care from the bed, I watched as Ally turned to her side, still naked but facing away. I bit my lip at the curve of her ass, but pulled myself from the sight and taking great care, edged my way down the stairs.

Frank lay slumped where we'd left him in the living room, the light off as he gently snored, our clothes still covering him and my damp underwear in his hand.

Feeling a pang of guilt at what he'd missed, I grabbed my top and skirt with care, leaving my underwear in his hand.

When he woke he'd be disoriented as hell and he'd know something had gone on, but he'd missed it all.

Leaning down in front of his face I stopped myself from kissing his forehead. Instead I stared, wondering if he really could be at the centre of why I'd been sent to this country. His street. With Ally.

His snore changed tone and I hurried to the kitchen. The bunch was still there and I leafed through each of the metal keys, finding the one matching the brand of the door lock I'd memorised, pulling it free from the ring.

I left, pushing the key to the inside pocket of my coat and crept upstairs, laying my clothes on a pile on top of my bag at the foot of the bed before turning off the lamp and covering myself and Ally with the quilt.

Tucking myself in, I shuffled up to Ally and felt her warmth as I spooned against her skin. She purred at my touch; I wanted so much for her to wake as I pressed at her back. I wanted a repeat, but my eyes refused to stay open, soon losing myself to sleep.

27

My first recollection was the pounding pressure in my head. Then movement beside me.

For a moment I flushed with panic, unable to recall who I'd see stirring in the bed with me.

Was it Frank? Had I done the deed? Would I be a different person in his eyes now?

Turning onto my side and opening my eyes, I caught sight of Ally squinting back with a smile tucked into the corner of her mouth. A deja vu moment, but no, this wasn't the same.

"Good morning," she said in her silky voice, only a little sleep hardened as the night flooded back.

I'd got the key and Ally helped me, although she had no clue.

"You were right, by the way?" she said, interrupting my thoughts as snapshots of last night flew across my view.

"About what?"

"Everything is more than fine down there," she said with her grin going wider and her eyebrows raising.

I burst out laughing as she reminded me of the conversation in her garden only days after we'd first met. Then the laughter dampened as I concentrated on the building memories.

Creeping down the stairs with no clothes on. Checking up on Frank and getting the key.

For a moment I panicked, until I remembered pushing it into my coat hanging in the under-stairs cupboard.

Ally shuffled closer and I could smell myself on her breath. For a short moment I wondered if she recognised her scent from my lips.

Dr Devlin's voice sprung into my head, asking those same questions he had during Selection. I wonder if I'd tell him the truth if he asked me again.

The thought vanished, as did the banging in my head with Ally's warm hand tracing my naked thigh. I relaxed to my back without conscious thought, my head still turned and gaze fixed on hers. My legs opened to let her fingers fill the space between them, my hand wandering across her body and hers reacted the same as I had, with my fingers tracing a mirror of her path to find her tuft of hair and that tender spot.

She closed her eyes and I followed suit, both of us letting out a gentle moan.

The door flew open and our fingers stopped. Our eyes darted wide to see Frank stood at the door, blinking towards us. In his left hand he still held the white underwear he'd gifted to me.

"What happened?" he said, squinting at the bed.

Ally left her hand in place as she spoke. "It was me, I'm afraid. I thought we all needed something to keep us awake, but it seems I might have put the wrong stuff in the champagne," she said.

I kept my eyes on him as he carried on blinking, his expression unsure of where to settle.

"Oh my god. All I can remember was you two kissing, then..." He looked at the fine material in his hand.

"They're mine," I said. "But you can keep them."

He looked up, giving an uncertain smile.

I bucked as Ally moved her finger, swinging like a pendulum from side to side. I replied in kind with a determination not to be the one who gave away the game we were playing under the covers.

"Did you pass out too?" Frank said with a hopeful look.

"Yes," we replied in unison.

"But you somehow managed to get up here."

"Just about," Ally said.

"I, I," he stuttered, rubbing his head with his hand before he realised he was still holding my underwear. "Oh my god. I can remember you getting undressed then I couldn't fight it any longer."

With the pressure building in my chest, her hand stopped when Frank spoke again, this time his tone decisive and business-like.

"Look, we'll pick this up again soon, but I got a call.

I've got to go to an important meeting. Cat, your car is outside when you're ready and Jeeves is downstairs. Al, get dressed, you need to drive."

Her fingers pulled away and I felt a sudden void, desperate for her touch again. I pulled my hand away just as she leafed open her side of the covers and, jumping from the bed, she put her fingers to her mouth, kissing the tip whilst Frank's eyes widened at the sight of her naked body.

As she moved towards him he turned to me with expectation, but I wasn't moving. His eyes near split wide open as Ally kissed him deeply, his brow furrowing for a moment as he licked his lips, watching as my smile turned to a grin.

28

Showered and changed into my jeans and t-shirt, I was in the car within half an hour. With a fleeting goodbye, Frank and Ally following me out into their car as I pulled away. Our paths went different ways as we hit the end of the long tree-lined driveway.

I wasn't sure if it was thoughts of the night before, her hands, her mouth all over me, or the pain killers Ally had passed over as we kissed one last time before leaving, but I felt enveloped in warmth, wrapped in comfort, my head filled with her smile as I half lay, half sat in the deep leather seat.

The feeling never left throughout the journey and as I trudged up the stairs, giving a waved hello to the family sat around for dinner, falling to the bed.

I'd slept for twelve hours that night, having woken at eleven, but still I fell into a warm deep sleep as my head touched the pillow.

I surfaced the following morning and set about my tasks with a vigour only slightly lacking from my normal energy. I was up by five, but bypassed the computer. I hadn't made a report in weeks, then again I had nothing to say and I knew their limited vocabulary already. No one could say I wasn't observing up close.

Lenart was up and in the kitchen with his coffee. I wished him a good morning and he asked me what I had to be so happy about. I felt like telling him. I almost blurted out that I'd fallen in love, but the words shocked me even as they formed silently in my head.

Could that be it?

Could that be the warm fuzzy feeling?

Lenart saw me drifting off and shot me back to the room.

"We need to talk tonight," he said with a stern voice. "Please be available for eight."

"What are we talking about?" I said, my voice soft.

"I'll tell you tonight," he said, pouring the hot coffee

down his throat before he turned, disappearing for the rest of the day.

I dismissed the conversation. What was the worst he could do?

I'd completed the bulk of the chores by the time Celina returned from taking the kids to school and she hovered by my side as I finished up the washing.

"Nice bra," she said as I folded the underwear now separated from its sibling.

"Thanks," I replied, offering nothing else. "Lenart wants to talk to me tonight. Do you know what that's all about?"

She didn't speak straight away, as if waiting for her courage to build.

"He thinks you're out too much." She held her hands in the air, palm towards me. "I keep telling him you're young, but he says you have a job to do."

"I've stayed out for three nights in total? I don't get it. Is there something wrong with my work?"

"No and I told him that, but he said my standards are too low."

"What do you think he'll do?"

"I don't know. I think he's going to see how the talk goes."

"Is he going to fire me?" I said, a genuine lack of concern rising through me.

"He might."

I shrugged.

"I'd miss you," I said, raising a pout towards her.

"I'd miss you too, but it might not come to that."

Moving toward me, she opened her arms and I turned, gripping her tight and taking in her comforting warmth. I couldn't help but think how different it was to when I touched Ally.

"So what's been going on these last few weeks?" she said as she took a few paces back to lean against the counter.

"What do you mean?" I replied.

"You've changed, and I don't mean in a bad way. You seem to be less about that," she said, pointing at the washing, "and more about you," with her finger toward my chest.

I held myself back from my instinct to tell her everything. I wasn't sure if I could say it out loud.

Celina got there first. "You've met someone, haven't you?" she said, her mouth in a wide, excited smile.

I nodded and looked down to hide my grin.

"I'm pleased for you. You might just be finding yourself at last."

"And so are they," I replied, beaming back at her.

I spent the rest of the morning on a run, then took the dog and watched number fifty-six. There was no sign of her, no sign of anyone.

For the rest of the afternoon I mooched around the house whilst finding excuses to go up the stairs and look out of the window and across the lawn.

I found reasons to go outside. I cleaned the windows, turning each moment to see if she headed my way. There was still no sign.

She didn't come at four o'clock, her sometimes normal time to take the dog for a walk. She wasn't around before Lenart came home at eight for the talk.

I could smell the alcohol on his breath. Celina was nowhere around. I had a vague memory she'd taken the children off somewhere, into town for a movie. He had me all to himself.

I promised myself if he tried anything he'd end up with broken bones.

He didn't pour himself a glass of whiskey, despite my offer. He sat in the front room on the edge of the chair and held his hand out, motioning for me to sit opposite.

"Do you want to be here?" he said, a hint of more than one whiskey on his voice.

I paused with intent. "What do you mean?" I said. It felt like I thought I should have when I was a teenager; the emotions I'd never experienced. I'd gone through a lot, but

I'd had no conversations like this with my parents. I'd been a good kid. Driven. I'd had no time to get into trouble.

"Do you want to be here doing what you're doing?"

"No," I said. "I think I'm too young to be looking after other people."

He nodded with a slow, solemn bow.

"I have my own ideas," I added.

"I understand. I'll speak with the agency and I'm sure they'll reassign you."

"Okay," I replied, not sure what the au pair agency would think of the request. "But let them know not to hurry. I might take some time off first."

His face flew into a picture of surprise. "What do you mean?"

"I think I'm going to get some space," I said. "Before I go someplace else."

"But you know what that means, don't you?" he said.

"Of course I do," I replied, but I really didn't know what he was talking about.

"Look, you shouldn't rush this. I'll give you a week. Have a think. I tell you what, take time out. Stay here, don't worry about us or the house. I won't say anything until next week. Okay?" he said, leaning forward.

"Okay," I replied, dragging out the word, but I couldn't help being concerned about why he was being so nice. Unless he wanted me to stay. Had I called his bluff?

At least now I had a week to myself, something I hadn't had for some time. I could do with some time to be me, time to do what I wanted to do, and I knew exactly how I wanted to spend it.

I pulled my coat on and headed out of the door, leaving Lenart sat in front of the TV.

It took a long time for the answer at the door, but the invite inside didn't. In the living room I asked if Ally was around, but she wasn't. I hoped I hid my disappointment.

Lenara said she was on business with Frank. She'd gone because she spoke German and could drive. I wasn't sure who she was trying to convince as she told me their usual interpreter had taken ill and Frank had drafted Alarica in at the last minute. No time to get a temp. No money for the extra expense.

"When is she likely to be back?"

"A week, I think?" she said, her voice vacant.

I felt the blood drain from my face; tears built in the corner of my eyes.

"Catarina, dear. I was going to ask anyway, but it was great you came around. Could you do me a favour and take the dog out for a walk? I know it's dark, but you don't seem to mind."

I nodded, barely hearing the words. I headed to the drawer underneath the table by the door and the dog came bounding after me as he heard the wood scraping under the table. As I clipped the lead on to his collar, Lenara met me at the door, handing over a bunch of keys.

"I'm going to be out when you get back. I'm staying with friends tonight. I don't like to be alone too much in this house. If you can just drop him back in and feed him. Keep the keys. If I'm not back can you do the same tomorrow?"

I nodded in reply, not able to push the words through my disappointment. I might leave this place for good and I wouldn't have a chance to find out if there was anything worth staying for.

The dog pulled me between the houses, showing no regard for my mood, my head facing down with the weight of my gloom. We were both glad when I let him off the lead as we entered the darkness.

We walked for what seemed like hours, and probably was, but I made no reference. I walked almost as far as the furthest I'd ever run, but my mood hadn't lifted. The growing cold finally turned me back.

Despite the chill, I walked slowly with my breath catching in the air as I emerged from the canopy. Darkness had fallen. Our driveway full; theirs empty. Only one car sat in the rest of the street, a few places down the road some way back. I'd never seen it before. Sometimes I wished I could turn off my senses.

Arriving at the house, I pushed in the front door key, almost laughing to myself. I should have told Lenara I didn't need another key, but then what would be the point of that?

Inside the house I pushed on the lights, drying the dogs paws on the towel they kept hidden away by the front door just for the purpose. Setting the dog's food in his bowl, I pushed the kitchen door closed to stop him from carrying food in his mouth and dropping it around the house.

While I waited for him to finish, I leant against the hallway wall, catching a fleeting shadow moving at the front door. I stared, but there was nothing there. Then the shadow moved again. This time I already had my gaze set in the direction.

Still, I jumped with a knock at the door. I stood frozen to the spot, a thought pulling into my mind that it might be Ally.

No. She would have her own key.

Despite my sense, I didn't look through the spy glass. Didn't push on the chain. Instead, I opened the door and watched as a tall, thin man stood there, his face wrapped with a brown unkempt beard only barely covering bald patches of missing growth.

His mouth was full of black teeth smiling back and in his bandaged right hand he pushed forward a long, wide knife.

29

My training forced me not to lash out and disarm the guy, despite this being my best opportunity, taking him by surprise with a furious show of my abilities.

The task flashed back into view. I remembered where I stood and who could be watching. This certainly was an interesting turn of events and the guy's appearance dragged me out of my teenager's mope, straight back into the zone.

In a flash I recalled the car down the road. I'd brushed it aside, almost uncaring.

"Who are you?" he said, his voice high and instantly recognised as the same guy who'd been refused entry to the Bukia's party.

"Aren't I meant to be the one asking?" I said, backing away down the corridor, trying to look scared.

"But I'm the one with the knife," he replied with his hand behind his back, pushing the door shut.

"I suppose," I replied. "I'm the girl next door. I mean, I live next door."

"Is there anyone else in? That girl they keep around?"

"Their daughter?" I replied, despite knowing who he referred to.

"No. The older one, the one that doesn't seem to have any purpose," he said, squinting in my direction as if he found it difficult to see.

"I'm the only one here. I just came to walk the dog and now he's eating," I replied, looking towards the closed door of the kitchen.

"Bad luck for you. Good luck for me," he said, still stepping forward and forcing me to back away.

I let my back slap hard against the closed door leading to the living room.

"What do you want? I don't know where they keep their money. It's not my house."

"I don't want money," he spat. "You're not trouble, are you?"

"No," I said, keeping my palms opened towards him.

"Good. Now turn around and put your hands behind your back," he hissed.

It was the moment for a decision. I could take him ten times over. He was slow and weary, his left hand bruised and riddled with scars. I could pull so many weapons from the tall tables along the hall; a plant pot, a framed painting.

I could grab the grandfather clock and push it down onto him. But his arrival was an opportunity I just couldn't miss.

Instead, I turned, watching the reflection in the framed picture's glass as I pushed my hands behind my back. I almost laughed. This guy was so lame.

He tucked the knife into his belt, almost cutting off a finger as he did.

He pulled a pair of zip ties from his coat pocket and tied my hands at my back, one around each wrist, both interlinked whilst I tried to clench my hands and make my wrists as big as possible, squealing as I felt the first touch of the plastic so he wouldn't pull any tighter.

No sooner than he'd pushed the last one home, he raised my arms up together, forcing me to push my shoulders forward to limit the pain. Still, I could stop it all, but instead I exaggerated my groan as he pushed me along the hall whilst clearly enjoying the sounds of my discomfort.

With confidence in his steps, he led me straight up the stairs, still forcing my torso forward.

Arriving on the landing he seemed not to know the layout upstairs, dragging me backwards with a tight hold around my arm as he flung open each of the doors.

He went to Ally's room first and I caught her scent as we entered. He headed straight to the cupboard, raking the towels out from the shelf. Not finding what he sought, he dragged me out to the hallway.

The main bathroom was next and he slapped bottles and potions from the shelves in the cupboards, then with more care, inspected the contents of the medicine cabinet, cursing each moment.

The master bedroom came after and he threw me facedown to the bed, rushing to the cupboard but grabbing me again when he couldn't find what he looked for.

Finally we reached the study, dragging me through the doors, sending a bolt of pain up my shoulders with a reaction I didn't need to exaggerate.

Shoving me towards the bookcase, I stumbled, catching my shoulder hard against the floor and I cried out with real pain when he kicked my legs, forcing me to pull them closed. As he slapped the lights on, I cursed him under my breath. He was very lucky he was doing me a favour, despite not knowing it.

"Stay in the corner and keep your fucking mouth shut. You better hope I find what I want or I'm having you as my compensation," he spat.

Without turning around, he ran to the back of the desk and wrenched open the drawers either side before tipping out the contents to the long blotter.

As I watched, I shuffled my back into the corner. Leaning against the bookcase I tried to let my shoulders relax while I busied my hands and within a few seconds I had the right cuff slipped off. I slid it back in, trying not to let the cuff tighten whilst I watched his growing frustration as he swiped the contents of each drawer to the carpet.

He'd run out of contents before he'd found what he searched for. Grumbling under his breath, he stepped around the desk to the wardrobe doors and pulled at the handles. They didn't move and he turned to me as I cowered against the wall.

"Where's the fucking key?" he shouted through dark, gritted teeth, swapping his look between me and the hole in the wood.

While he'd been searching, I'd examined the door in more detail.

"I don't live here. I have no idea," I said, adding a quiver to my voice.

I didn't say that if I'd known then you'd be on the floor with your hands around your back and your face covered in bruises.

He returned to the desk, rifling once more through the strewn contents of the drawers, pushing the debris of everyday office life to the floor with his face growing redder with each alternating sweep of his hands. He knocked a heavy paperweight to the floor, a lump of glass which seemed to have some creature suspended inside, bouncing from the carpet to hit my shin.

Huffing in pain, I forced down the reaction so not to draw his attention. I needn't have worried because moments later a dark, toothy grin told me he'd uncovered something to prick his interest.

Pulling the key from the pile, he glanced in my direction.

I wouldn't let him down prematurely. He'd realise soon enough that the key, albeit the right size, wouldn't pass into the dark keyhole.

As he found out, he threw the key down at his back. It glanced off the wall close to my face as he banged his fists on the doors, grabbing at the ornate contours of the wooden detailing as if he'd pluck it right off its hinges with brute force alone. Only when he looked like he would explode with rage did he stop moving, stepping to the side to peer down at the low centre panel which slipped to reveal a digital keypad in the middle.

The buttons were like from a phone with numbers from one to three across the top, then three more rows with the rest. Each number, except for nine, also represented a set of three letters. He twisted a glance in my direction and I shrugged back, raising my eyebrows. What was he expecting from me?

He turned back to the door and jabbed his fingers at the first four buttons in sequence. After waiting a moment when nothing happened, he carried on punching in the digits of the linear sequence, leaving an expectant pause between each. After the seventh digit, a low bass alert came from somewhere in the panel and a small red LED lit above the keypad.

Peering closer, I could see another two unlit in the line.

Twisting toward me, I shrugged once more in reply. He'd at least figured out he'd tapped in the wrong answer, but did he really think I knew the sequence?

I did. As soon as I'd heard the tone on the seventh number, the answer became obvious.

He punched in another set, this time appearing to jab in sequence and on the seventh press the tone repeated and the second light turned red. Scowling at me, he soon snapped back with his finger hovering with indecision over each of the numbers.

Was he expecting divine intervention?

Moving his finger, he seemed as if he would try one last shot. Before he could, I whispered the numbers just loud enough for him to hear.

Two. Five. Two. Seven. Four. Two. Two.

They spelled Alarica.

I gave another shrugged reply when he squinted back.

"If this goes red, then you're going to have a much worse day."

Facing the doors and with care, he punched in the numbers. Each of the LEDs turned green, and the doors released, opening outward of their own accord with light pouring from behind to cast him in silhouette.

"What the fuck?" he whispered under his breath, then slipping the cuff again and rising silently to my feet, I smashed the paperweight into the back of his head.

30

He fell to the floor like a sack of shit, or as an unconscious body does when it no longer receives any messages from the brain, the knife clattering forward to the floor ahead.

Rubbing my wrists, I leaned over him, pulling his head up and slipping up each eyelid with a finger. He gave no signs of consciousness and I let his head bump to the carpet, knowing I didn't have to worry about him for a little while.

Picking up the knife, I turned my attention forward and the hole where the light streamed up from; the space where the floor of the wardrobe should have been.

Taking tentative steps, I saw raw concrete walls finished only with what appeared to be a coat of magnolia. Before I went any further, I examined the door frame, catching sight of the tiny sensor contacts telling of an alarm ringing somewhere.

Speeding my steps, I let the knife fall through the missing floor as I watched its downward path past the metal ladder and bright lights fixed to the shaft wall. With a great clatter, it came to rest with a sharp echo.

I turned to the man as good as dead for the next few minutes, then looked down to the knife and let my foot settle on the top rung. Guessing I had such little time, I rushed down the steps until my feet hit the floor.

I landed in a room with its walls finished the same as the shaft; raw concrete painted the same not cream, not white colour, but somewhere in between. In the room stood a wide dark-wooden desk, not unlike the one above; behind it sat a large leather arm chair with an over-stuffed couch to the side filling the length of the wall.

My gaze fell to the desk again and my heart jumped as I saw my underwear from that night, dispelling any doubt at his involvement. With time against me and despite the race of my mind, I forced myself to continue turning on the spot to face a glass door, through which I saw a long, brightly lit tunnel reaching out to vanish to a point in the distance.

Completing the turn I came face to face with a grid of four by four television screens, the desk and couch both lined up to point in their direction.

Staring at the screens, I paused for a moment, watching the detail of warehouse-sized rooms on each. Inside were beds, or trolleys, most occupied with figures, people laying down. The scene conjured that of a hospital, right down to the cables and tubes spiralling off to monitors at the side of each bed. Heart traces showed on those monitors close enough to the cameras. It was as if I could almost hear their beeps.

I watched as nurses, or orderlies, milled between the beds. Occasionally someone would stop beside one and fiddle with settings on a small machine or exchange a hanging IV bag.

My view continued over each of the screens until I caught sight of what appeared to be an operating theatre, the first of two. On the last I saw an operation in full swing and I stared on at what seemed to be an amputation of a leg, when the patient suddenly moved to the side, fighting against binds with a power saw cutting through their leg.

I flinched, my stomach contracting, ready to hurl its contents to the floor.

The nurses to the side moved in from the edges to force the person down, but rather than stopping the procedure, they held him firm.

These were no movie images, no horror films as I'd first thought; the time and date in the corner told me they were CCTV and, at a guess, were showing what was going on at the end of the long tunnel.

The men in white coats were not healing these people; the blood-splattered aprons were not from surgical precision.

As my thoughts crashed and clattered together, a noise above cut through the questions.

I turned back to the screens. The bottom left showed two cars pulled up outside fifty-six and three of the football players I'd seen at the party were running up the drive and towards the front door. The next image rotated between different views of the inside of the house; Ally's bedroom, the bathroom, the stairs.

Now I knew why Frank had made the house out of bounds for their games.

Picking up the knife, I climbed up the ladder with my heart pounding in my chest and body numb as if I'd just woken from a thousand-year sleep. Above I could hear the front door open, but I had to slow my ascent; the stomp of my feet on the metal rattled like I was ringing my own echoing alarm bell.

Soon at the top with my head just below the level, I drew a deep breath and smashed my forehead into the concrete wall to the sound of footsteps on the stairs just above. Stars sparkled across my view and I could only just hold on to the rung. Somehow I climbed out, stumbling over the fallen guy who lay not moving.

With just enough time to push my hand through the tie wrap, pulling it tight with the other, I felt myself reeling forward, the stars building to lines as I closed my eyes and let go of consciousness.

31

I woke with a face hovering over mine. A guy I recognised from the party.

For a moment I thought it was still the first time I'd been to the house and I listened for the sounds of conversation in the background. Maybe I'd drunk too much. Maybe he would help me get back to my bed, but then the sharp sting at my forehead told me why I lay on the floor.

I watched the guy's lips move, but the words were only just coming into focus and I couldn't quite understand what he was saying. The only thing I knew for certain was the gratitude at my hands being free again.

Reaching out to touch my hand to my forehead, I watched the guy, his image suddenly fuzzy as I made contact.

He winced, drawing my hand away. "How do you feel?" he said, his words sounding a little slurred, but I could at least understand them now.

I turned to the side, unable to speak as the contents of my stomach flowed.

"What's happening?" was all I could get out as I saw the doors close and the guy next to me leave the room.

"There was an intruder. Do you remember anything?" another voice said with a mixture of concern and authority.

"I… remember… him," I said, just retaining enough sense to cower. "Is he gone?"

"Yes, he's gone. You're safe," the new voice said.

"Are you the police?"

"Kind of. We work for Mr Bukia. You're safe now. Can you tell me what you remember?"

I waited a moment, letting my stomach settle.

"He forced those doors and I head-butted him. A little too hard, I think." My hand went halfway to the lump on my forehead before the only guy in the room pushed it gently away. "I should get home," I said and tried to stand, but my legs wouldn't hold my weight and I collapsed into the arms of the guy collecting me up, cradling me with his chest like pillows. I watched as he walked to another room and lay me down on a bed.

"The doctor is on his way," were the last of his words I heard before I drifted into darkness.

***

I woke to light filling the room. Natural light.

I turned to see the canula in the back of my hand and a clear tube disappeared somewhere I daren't follow for the sake of my stiff neck.

Ally sat on the edge of the bed, beaming a wide grin.

I smiled back and she dropped the book to the floor, leaning closer.

"She's alive," she said in a quiet voice before she leant further and kissed my cheek.

"You're back," I said, my voice weak and dry, the words forcing a squint at the pounding in my head.

"You hit that bastard real hard. Here, the doctor said you might want these pain killers when you woke."

I let her help me sit up, drinking the water as she handed over the cup, then knocking back the pills without question.

"How's your vision?"

"Only one of you, I'm afraid," I replied with a gentle laugh.

"One's enough, isn't it?" she replied, wearing on a scowl.

"More than enough," I replied. "Did he get anything?"

"Only what he deserved," she said, her expression stern.

Staring into her eyes I took warmth from her smile, but the images from the screens dissolved into view. Fear rose up from my core, not for myself, but for Ally. A desperation built for those people still down there.

I'd only known her for such a short time, but there was no chance she could have any idea what that monster was doing. She had no idea who she'd been sharing a bed with.

"What's wrong?" she said with a frown bunching on her forehead.

"I'm just remembering, that's all."

"Tell me what happened. Tell me everything. It'll help. Did he do anything to you?" she said, looking me up and down despite being completely covered with a duvet.

"No. This was my doing," I said. "He opened those doors and I saw my chance."

"Do you know what he was trying to get? Did he say anything?"

I paused as I heard footsteps outside the room. The door opened and Frank appeared with a wide, surprised look on his face.

"No. He said he was looking for something. I went out cold as I head butted him."

Ally made space for Frank to sit on the edge of the bed beside her and he leaned in, stroking my cheek with the back of his hand.

With my skin crawling at his touch, it was all I could do not to flinch away.

"Thank you," he said. "Thank you for protecting my home."

"I've got to go home now," I replied and pulled myself out of the bed. They tried to stop me, almost pleading with me to stay for a few hours more or to have something to eat, but I insisted, only conceding to let one of their guys walk me between the two houses.

After telling Celina the bare minimum, I spent the rest of the day laying in my own bed; a bed that I'd have for only a few days more as my mind raced over those images. Those scenes on the CCTV monitors.

With hourly checks by Celina, the pain calmed, but still I couldn't bring myself to eat. Between those images and the thoughts of Ally with that man next door, I spent much of my effort stopping myself from bringing up whatever remained of my last meal.

After a few hours I was overjoyed to hear the knock at the door and just as Celina was telling Ally I was sleeping, I headed slowly down the steps.

Celina looked up, raising her eyebrows and tilting her head to the side but left us to it.

"How's the head?" Ally said. She stood at the front door, squinting up the stairs much like Celina had, holding her hand at the frame to stop the dog from pulling her arm from her socket.

"Fine now," I lied. "The headache's gone but the bruise is going to be special."

"You up to a walk?" she said, tipping her head outside.

I joined her without nodding, not trusting the movement.

We walked slowly for a long time with neither of us speaking, the silence almost comforting, Ally realising how my head must have made me feel.

It wasn't until we turned back I spoke for the first time.

"When can we meet up again?" I said, raising my eyebrows but lowering them again as a flash of pain reminded me of my injury. "I really want to be with you again. Soon."

"Me too. So does Frank, but he's only just getting over what I did with the champagne."

I bit my lip, holding back the words I wanted to say.

"This weekend?" she said.

"Okay, but do we have to wait that long, you know, for you and me?" I replied.

She giggled, circling her arm through mine and pulling me close. I wanted to get her alone for longer than it took to walk the dog so I could tell her everything and then give her time to calm back down so we could plan what to do next.

"Frank would kill me if we did anything without him, especially the first time. He still thinks we passed out and didn't do…" She paused, a grin showing her bright white teeth. "You know. What we did."

I released from her grip, grabbed the sides of her head and pulled her face close to mine, kissing her deep. She pushed towards me, pressing hard until we had to come up for air.

Getting her breath back, she spoke. "I'll see what I can do."

When I got home, I had the house to myself and after double checking Celina had left, I powered up the family computer and tapped out the details of what I'd seen. I made sure I added all the previous information I couldn't remember if I'd previously reported.

The response came back only a few seconds later.

Hold...

I waited, for the first time not disappointed when I hit the enter key.

I didn't have to wait long and I saw more text in their reply than all their messages received so far.

There was no registered clinic of that kind for two hundred miles of where I was sitting. There was a doctor working for his company, but he'd been removed from the medical register five years ago after being prosecuted for unethical experimentation on vulnerable people. His name was Francis Burchet.

I deflated as the reply ended with the familiar words.

Instructions:

Observe. Report.

I was about to close down the connection when another line appeared.

Report back within 24 hours.

I cleared my footprint of messages and hit the power button, trying to hold myself back from slamming my fist onto the desk, taking solace that tomorrow they may have made some decision.

32

With a tap at the door the following morning, I held a box the same size as the first. As Celina had handed it over, she'd asked me if I was okay or something similar. I shook my head or nodded, I can't remember which, but she left me alone either way.

I lingered on the ground floor when I heard her on the phone; she was telling someone there might be something wrong as she spoke with a concerned edge to her voice. I didn't stick around, the box burning in my hands.

Inside was another complete set of the white underwear. The note in her hand made me smile at first, blotting out the darkness choking my heart. Anger brewed inside me, growing as I read on, but at least I knew I could tell her soon.

We'd run away. I'd get her away from here as soon as I could, then I'd call it in. They'd arrange for a tactical nuke or something, sending the army to rescue those still alive, then blow the place sky high, taking him away to reflect on the torture he'd directed.

The note told me she'd pulled it off. He'd needed little convincing when she said how I eager I'd been and he'd cleared a slot in his diary for this afternoon. I would meet her and the car, take a short drive then get straight to it.

I knew the drill; she hadn't needed to tell me to wear the replacement for what sat on his underground desk.

I tried to stop myself thinking it over. I just had to get the moment over then on the drive back we'd go somewhere else while he was busy. A bar or somewhere.

I buried myself in the ritual of preparing for the deed. Bathing. Preening. Washing my hair.

Full of pain killers and excitement to see her, I bounded towards her house at the allotted time, no sooner or later than planned.

Ally met me at the door with the car already outside. My mood lifted even further at her sight, pushing away the last of the darkness which had wrapped around me.

Slapping me on the ass as I climbed in the car, sparks flew from the sensation as she bounced to my side, her lips clamping to mine as I felt the car move.

We writhed in pleasure, not even bothering to stop for a drink. Her hands roved over my neck, moving down to my breasts and ass while mine took their own route over her silky clothes, our tongues chasing around the other's mouth.

The car stopped, the door opening too soon. I'd lost track of time, but not so much that I knew we were still local.

Panting for breath, I looked on at the driver. He held the door but looked away as the metal of the car framed the door of a roadside motel.

I felt my heart palpitate, but Ally's hands were gentle at my back, urging me out of the car.

Stumbling and still in a light-headed daze, she took my hand as the car door closed and drove away.

Ally used a key card from her small purse and opened the door to show the wide, darkened room with candles flickering from every flat surface.

My breath stole as I caught sight of the large bed with no duvet, just white sheets stretched tight and plump pillows at the head. Candles stood on the window, the bedside tables and on every other surface as I took in the room.

With the door closed at my back I thought for a moment; it was my chance to talk to her before he came, but then my unfocused gaze caught, as did my breath, when I saw his clothes piled neatly on the floor by the wooden dresser.

Following Ally's lead, she pulled off her coat and threw it to the floor at the side of the door, mine landing on top.

I turned as she did, looking to the bathroom as the door opened and watched as Frank stood with steam from the shower at his back, wrapped in a white towelling robe.

I felt myself almost gag as I saw him, remembering the images on the screens.

He opened his palms as he walked to the bed. Ally took both my hands and turned me towards her.

The bile calmed as she leant forward, kissing me with the same vigour as before and our tongues furiously mingled. Her hands were at the hem of my top, which she soon had over my head. Her fingers dropped my skirt to the floor and I stepped out of the material, her hands running up and down my back and over my ass as I pulled her top off to reveal her scarlet bra. In double time I had it over her head, not letting her mouth free as she pulled the bra straps from her arms.

My fingers moved to her nipples and she turned me by ninety degrees.

Frank lay on the bed, sitting with his back slouched against the pillows. With one leg bent, his knee in the air, the towel lay on the floor to the side. In his right hand he held himself. It was massive; so much bigger than I'd expected. And circumcised. Another surprise.

Ally let loose a small giggle.

Somehow I was already separating the person from the body. Maybe it was Ally's kisses on my neck, or the freedom of my nakedness.

I pulled in a deep breath as she let my knickers down to my ankles. She didn't need to push too much to get my legs open, her fingers brushing over my mound before diving inside me.

I almost let go there and then, my eyes closing as she played. A sharp breath pulled in when she withdrew.

"She's ready. Oh my god, she's ready," Ally said with such enthusiasm.

I nodded, despite my insides screaming at my actions. I was ready and I wanted it so bad. My head told me just not with him.

Here, yes. Now was the right time, with Ally watching. Oh my god.

But could I really be thinking about having sex with this monster?

33

Ally pulled me from my questioning, pecking me on the cheek. Frank moved off the bed to stand at Ally's side as she ushered me to take his place on top of the mattress, which I did without putting up a fight and touched down in his warmth.

Both Frank and I stared on as Ally slowly undid her skirt, sliding her knickers down her legs. I shared my gaze between them as I lay on my back, my legs spreading as I watched them turn to each other, him greedily kissing at her mouth as she grabbed hold of him, stroking up and down whilst he arched his back in pleasure.

Oh my god, it was going to happen.

I looked to Ally and then to Frank. They'd stopped kissing and had both turned toward me. Her with a sweet, knowing grin, eager for me to have my experience. Him like I was his prey, caught in a trap.

He placed his knees to the bed, crawling towards me with his dick springing up and down, the end slick with liquid dripping from the tip. Our eyes locked and my breath caught as I saw the same expression hanging on the face of the driver of the empty coach.

A flashback pulled me to the view of the diner. The coach full of people; young and old as they waved at me with the coach moving off. Then the return journey; the seats empty.

Despite feeling the bed moving and his shape coming towards me, all I could think of was that I'd seen plenty of full coaches heading one way towards the factory, but never had I seen a coach full of people heading in the other direction.

The coaches arrive full. The coaches leave empty.

They were still there. They were the people I'd seen strapped to the beds.

I took a deep breath and I closed my eyes. I could feel his warmth near me, his torso touching mine. His dick slapped between my legs and I yelped with my arms springing outward. My left hand caught at the side to the sound of glass smashing, followed by a rush of air I soon realised could only mean one thing.

With a sudden brightening of the room, Ally screamed and Frank jumped from the bed. Ally's hand took mine, pulling me up and I turned to see the bed alight just as she pulled me away.

I'd caught the candle, the wax spilt, soaking into the sheet to make a giant wick. Ally and I backed up to the corner of the room, coughing and spluttering. We held each other tight as Frank first threw the ice bucket over, then sprayed champagne, killing the flames.

He turned back toward us, his face calming and his dick limp.

"Are you okay?" he said, looking at Ally, then me.

"I'm fine," she replied.

"I'm so sorry," I said. There was a knock at the door and Frank rushed to the spy hole.

"Everything's fine," he shouted through the door. "Just a little accident. Everything's under control."

He walked to a small bag and pulled a hip flask from inside, unscrewed the lid and took a sip, then passed it to Ally.

I took it from her as she'd finished her gulp.

Frank blew air out. "That was close."

"What a mood killer," Ally said, grabbing at our clothes and passing mine over. The room stank of burnt plastic. I pulled on my things.

"I'm really sorry," I said.

"It was an accident," Frank replied. "We'll do this someday," he said, looking back at me.

I forced a smile and nodded.

"I'm sorry," I repeated as Ally rubbed at my shoulders.

"Don't worry, but we better get back home," she said, and I nodded, cowering as she handed over my coat.

Frank kissed each of us on the cheek as we headed out of the door and the waiting car.

Relaxing into the leather seat, I took a deep breath.

"Ally, can I tell you something in private?" I said,

switching my look to the driver. I couldn't wait any longer.

"Of course," she said, pushing a button on the door handle and a dark pane of glass rose between the driver and the passenger compartments. "What is it?"

"I saw something," I said, but Ally didn't react. "I saw something when that guy was ransacking your house."

Her eyelids gave the tiniest of movements.

"What did you see?" she said, her voice low.

"When he opened those doors in the study..."

"The wardrobe?" she replied.

"It's not a wardrobe," I said, taking her hand in mine. "There was a ladder going down through the house, going underground." I tightened my grip on her hand as she reeled back in surprise.

"A ladder?"

I watched as tears welled in the corner of her eyes.

"Metal rungs set into the wall. A ladder that went down into a room, to a tunnel."

"You went down there?" she said, wiping the corner of her eyes with the backs of her hands.

"It's okay," I said, trying to reassure her. "When I hit the guy with the paperweight," I watched as she flinched back as I spoke, "he dropped the knife down there and I didn't feel safe without it. In case he woke up."

"I thought you said you headbutted him?"

I shook my head.

"But you went down to the tunnel?"

"Yes. And I saw things."

"What things?" she said, leaning forward and drawing in a deep breath.

"They had these CCTV monitors. The house. The drive. They were all on there. And there were these other rooms."

"What rooms? What did you see?" she said slowly, leaning back to the leather.

"There were patients in beds, on trolleys. It's some medical facility."

"Oh right," she said, shaking her head. "I guess it's something to do with the factory?"

"But that's not everything."

"Go on," she said slowly.

"There were operating theatres. People having procedures. Or tests."

"Okay. It doesn't sound like anything to worry about."

I held her hand tight. "The people were still awake," I said, looking straight into her eyes. "Ally, the coaches come in full of women and kids, most of which are disabled, but they leave empty. They were testing something on them. I'm sure."

"Oh my god," she said, her eyes wide.

"Are you sure they weren't films?" she said with her hand over her mouth.

"No, they weren't. They'd be illegal. I can't even begin to tell you what was going on."

She hugged me close. "We must tell Frank."

I pulled away, but still held her by the shoulders at arm's reach, looking deep into her eyes.

"No, we can't. He's a part of it."

"No. What do you mean? He can't be."

"The entrance was in his study," I said, my eyes wide. "Do you remember the white knickers I was wearing the night we…?" I said, nodding towards her.

She grew a grin. "The pair you weren't wearing, you mean."

"Yes, those. They were on the desk down there."

"Oh my god," she said. The smile vanished. "I don't… I won't believe it. This can't be true."

"It's true," I said, grabbing her towards me as she struggled, tears streaming down to the tops of my arms.

"What are you going to do?" she said in my ear.

"We'll get away. We'll get far away, call the police. I know people that can help."

"You know people? What do you mean?"

"Don't worry," I said. "We'll be safe." I held her in my arms, pulled her tight.

As I looked at the window, the car passed the turn-off for our little estate.

I let Ally go. "He's going the wrong way," I said, pointing out of the window.

"It's okay. I told him to take us some place quiet."

I nodded, despite not recalling when she'd said anything to the driver. I shook away the thought, watching as each of the bars in the strip malls wound by the window.

We stopped at a fifth place; a low building with neon signs bright in the dusk. With the carpark deserted, we doubled the patron count as the driver left us to it.

I ordered two double scotches with no ice as Ally headed to the toilets. The sharp oak vapour reminded me of the tainted smell on my clothes.

I took a booth and Ally came back, her questions firing at me as she sat opposite, downing the drink.

"You set that fire deliberately, didn't you?"

"I had to. I couldn't go through with it. Not with him. I wanted to with you, but not with him after what I've seen."

She looked around the room and back at me, pushing two fingers in the air at the barkeep.

"You should have said something before, in the car on the way there."

"I was going to, but you carried me off to another place," I said, leaning towards her, my hand going across the table. "I want to be with you. I want to take you some place safe."

She stared back, her eyes seeming to long for my touch, but she kept her hands by her side. Her gaze stayed fixed on mine as the new drinks arrived.

"Drink that," she said, when the bartender arrived back behind the bar. "You're going to need it."

I took the first drink down in one, shivering as the fumes burned at the back of my nose.

"You'll come with me?" I said, pushing my hand across the table for a second time.

She curled her bottom lip into her mouth and gave a

shallow nod. "Where will we go?" she said, downing the rest of her drink.

"Anywhere. Wherever. As far as we can."

She raised her fingers in the air and I shook my head.

"Not for me. I need to keep a clear head for the journey," I said, lifting myself up from the seat.

Unfolding a bill, I changed it for a roll of coins at the bar and headed through the double doors to the toilets and the payphone.

I recognised the faces of the two guys stood at the end of the short corridor. I recognised the face of the guy moving to stand at my back as I turned.

Through the porthole behind him I saw Ally staring out of the tall windows into the distance as pain showered across my skull and the world faded to black.

34

I woke in a hotel room a few storeys high, if the dark view out of the tall windows could be believed. I had no idea in what part of town.

Sitting upright in a dining chair in the middle of the room, a pair of empty large double beds nestled to my right. I couldn't see a screen but behind me a TV blared with some sport involving commentators shouting at each other.

My legs wouldn't move; something held them firm to the chair legs, my hands bound at my back.

There was someone, more than one someone in the room by the sounds of the slow, relaxed breath just heard between the pause of excitement from the TV.

Peering down, I could see I wore the same low-cut top and skinny skirt I'd blacked out in, the tang of smoke rising to my nostrils.

The TV clicked off, but no words followed. A door opened and I felt another presence.

Frank came around from my side, squinting at me, sizing me up. Was he trying to figure if there had been a mistake somewhere along the line?

I took away any ambiguity.

"You monster," I said in the lowest voice I could muster. I didn't need to hide my emotion. I'd none for him.

I watched as his eyes relaxed and a deep grin turned his lips upward.

He stared for a great while, then took a deep breath. "I'm sorry it had to be like this," he said.

I believed him, but only because he wanted what I had.

"You're not denying it?" I said. I wanted to hear it in his own words.

"What do you want me to say?" he said, but he didn't give me a chance to reply. "Do you want me to apologise for trying to find the end of pain? Do you want me to apologise for helping to end all future suffering?"

"Your cause is noble. Your methods not so."

"Giant leaps can be made if some people just make a few sacrifices."

"Sounds like something out of the mouth of a Nazi," I replied, raising my brow.

"No. They were trying to build a super race. They were trying to build a super solider. I don't care who benefits. Young or old, black or white." The corner of Frank's mouth rose in a sneer as he shook his head.

"As long as they have the money?"

Frank laughed, raising his eyebrows. "We live in a capitalist world, my dear Cat."

"I don't think the guy who broke into your house had the same idea," I replied shifting in the seat.

"You figured him out. Well done." His smile grew.

"He was one of your early patients, wasn't he?"

"He was," he replied, slowly nodding.

"You left him without being able to feel pain."

"Remember back to your school days. No one gets it right first time. Science is all about experimentation. Trial and error."

"Tell me what he wanted?"

Frank shook his head. "This isn't a question-and-answer session."

"What is it then?"

"A goodbye."

"What did he want?" I repeated.

Frank smiled and turned to the lights in the streets spreading out across the alien view from the windows.

"He was a little premature. He thought I'd finished my work. He thought I'd had a breakthrough."

"He thought you kept the cure at home."

"Yes. We're close, but not there yet. He's pain free now, I'm sure you'll be pleased to hear," he said with his cheeks bunching.

"How many more coaches full of women and children will you need before you get a breakthrough?"

Frank turned back to face me with a forced grin as he

leant down close to my face, but not close enough that I could reach him with a swing of my forehead.

He took a deep breath. "You were so promising, Cat. I was going to offer you a job. I would have looked after you. Set you up for life. Now I'm afraid it all has to come to an end."

"I don't care what you do to me. Where's Ally? What have you done with her?" I heard the door open and could smell her sweet perfume before she came around the chair and stood by his side, dismissing a hope of her tied at my back and in the same position, but reversed.

As I smelt her enter the room, I hoped to see mascara lines down her red puffy face from the tears she couldn't stop from flowing. The other half expected what I saw; she was perfect. Dressed in tight black leggings hugging the muscular curve of her thighs I'd known for a short time, with a baggy short T-shirt on top. She wore no makeup and I couldn't sense any lingering smoke.

Worst of all, she wore a bright, wide smile.

Rage built up inside me, but I directed inwards at the small tears running down my cheeks.

"I'll miss you, Cat," she said, tucking her arm behind Frank's.

"So sweet," he said. "We could have been amazing together, us three."

Squinting, I tried as best I could to hold back the emotion, turning away as Ally spoke.

"We better get going," she said. "I can't bear to watch these things."

I felt my heart ripped from my chest and it lay under her heels as she ground it into the floor.

Had any of it been real? But then again, did that matter now?

It was over, but I couldn't let go just like that.

Why had I let this happen? The warning signs had been there. I knew how much of a great liar she could be. I knew how capable she was of putting up a convincing front. But still

I let it happen.

I looked up as I watched their feet disappear around to my back, replaced either side with three pairs of men's slip-on shoes and the football players with their jackets off, a Beretta holstered under each arm over a crisp white shirt. Each wore lurid grins, growing as Frank's voice came from behind.

"Oh boys, be careful. She knows people," he laughed, as I heard his voice get quieter with the distance. "Oh and I almost forgot. Don't let the poor thing die a virgin. She's still on the boil from earlier."

It was Ally's voice I heard next.

"Three times over," she said, as the door muffled their laughter.

35

Lost for words, I looked to the carpet. I felt as if a wild animal had ripped me open and devastated my insides.

Numb. Destroyed. I couldn't think. I couldn't do anything but sit in the chair.

I could only just lift my head as the trio laughed, their jokes turning to arguments about who would go first.

I recognised one of the laughs, but I summoned no will to move as fingers ran roughly through my hair, not flinching as each took turns to paw at my breasts.

I watched the left-hand bed as they discarded holsters, flinging shirts on top and trousers next; their hunger more important than the creases.

I let silent laughter leave my lips when I realised they would have to untie me if they were to have any chance of achieving their objective. I let their voices charge my anger.

"How do you want to do this?" said a deep voice at my back, the voice of the guy who'd found me unconscious in the study; the gentle arms that laid me to rest with such care.

"Fucking untie her and shove her on the bed," another said more urgently, somewhere further behind.

"I mean, front or back. Do you want to see her face as you do it?" the first guy said.

"Shit yeah. Untie her arms, too. You can hold her down as I break the seal," he said, laughing.

The other two didn't argue. Pressure pulled at my wrists as whatever bound me loosened, replaced with hands wrapping tight, pulling my arms towards the floor.

Another crouched at my feet, the guy from the study again. As he went to his knees he leant forward, pushing his head to my lap and took a big draw of breath.

"Fucking come on," a new voice said. Nate. "Get on with it."

The guy looked up at me and stared into my eyes as he spoke in a softened voice.

"Look. Just take it for what it is. It'll soon be over," he

said, as if to reassure me, then put his head back down to my knees and picked at the knots by my ankles.

It wasn't long before I felt another presence at my side and a cold steel blade resting against my neck.

A deep voice spoke slowly at my ear. "Do as we tell you and you might actually enjoy this. Do anything else and I'll fuck you with the knife when I'm finished. You understand?"

I nodded as hard as I could without pushing against the blade.

"Are you going to let us do this the easy way?" he said.

I nodded again and felt the pressure release from my arms and the guy at my feet release, backing off as he looked towards me. The metal had gone from my throat. I sat still.

"Now stand, but no quick movements," the same voice said.

I stood.

"Move to the bed."

I turned and for the first time I took in the room and the faces of the other two guys; I was right. Nate stood next to another guy I'd seen at the party. Neither had been at the hotel when I shot the guy protecting their boss. None of them had seen me in action, but would probably have heard about it.

Each of them stood in black boxers with black socks pulled high. Two were tenting out towards me, but Nate had his hand down his front, rubbing himself up and down.

Gulping for show, or that's what I told myself, I drifted towards the empty bed.

"Now take off your clothes," Nate said, his voice breathy.

My hands went to the hem of my top.

"Skirt first," came another equally breathy voice, but I couldn't tell which of them spoke..

My face impassive, I moved my hands down the curve of my back, dug underneath my shirt and both hands found the clip.

"Slower," Nate snapped.

My fingers replied, edging forward with micro movements. I gripped either side and let the hooks separate, fingers tracing down to find the zipper. I heard deep breaths, but they weren't getting closer. I let my fingers pull at the zip, the teeth separating in slow motion. It came to a stop and I let go, the thin fabric dropping to the floor.

"Turn around." Nate again.

I did as I was told and turned away from them.

"Bend forward," came the first voice again. "Over the bed," it said, and I did.

I felt my heart flutter, my mood woken with a spike of adrenaline. They hooted and hollered behind me, deep breaths pulling in. I thought at that moment one of them would grab out, pull the fabric to the side and the deed would be done.

"Wait," came Nate's voice, the word not directed to me. He was holding someone back and they seemed to obey the command. For now. "Turn around and do the top," he said again.

I stood up straight, turned around and took a deep breath as I grabbed the hem.

"Slowly," Nate added.

I could hear fabric moving. I slowed, letting the top come to just below my bra. I looked up and saw they were no longer hiding away, their underwear to the floor and standing proudly pointing toward me. They were ready.

I looked at the guy with the knife for permission. He nodded as I pulled the material higher, twisting it as the hem rubbed my bra strap. It caught, as I expected. Still, I pulled with my gaze locked to the guy with the knife. He looked red and swollen, like he wouldn't be able to hold on much longer.

"I'm stuck," I said as soft as I dared.

"Help her out," he said, motioning with the knife to Nate still pleasuring himself.

Grinning as he heard the command, Nate pulled his hand from his dick and took a slow step forward.

I licked my lips and he licked his, mirroring my gesture. I turned away, presenting myself by bending over ever so slightly. He ran his hand across my back just above my knickers. I could feel his hardness touching me as he stroked the small of my back until his hands reached the tangle at the strap.

As I felt the material separate, I turned slowly until I was a breath from his face. He smiled as I pulled one arm and then the next from my top and threw the fabric towards the knife guy, landing it at his feet.

As he bent to pick up the top, I brought my knee to bear on Nate's crotch, the cap smashing his spheres into the base of his stiff dick.

The guy with the knife took a second to realise where the pained sound had come from and why his buddy had doubled on the floor, screaming but with no sound coming out.

He dropped my top and lunged forward. The other guy hadn't moved as he went out of view, hurling myself face down onto the other bed, my hands darting under the piled clothes with a Beretta pulling from the first leather holster.

I'd won the race, the safety off before the knife man completed his manoeuvre and the guy from the study had even reacted.

"Sorry, boys, I've got a headache."

I didn't need to shoot. I didn't need to shout. They followed my every direction as they lined up, kneeling and facing the wall, dragging their fallen colleague with them as I dressed.

"What are you going to do?" the guy who'd had the knife said, his features sullen.

"Now my turn for fun. I want to watch you suck both their dicks."

All three turned towards each other then back to me, glaring at the gun.

"You're kidding, right?" the guy who'd had the knife said.

I picked up a pillow and took a step closer.

"Of course," I said. I leaned the pillow into his torso

and pushed the Beretta in as deep as I could before pulling the trigger. Two more shots came not long after.

They panicked less than I thought they would, the sound only a little louder than a suppressor. I let the pillow drop to the floor on top of the last guy's body. How sad they looked in just their socks.

I wiped the gun of my prints and pulled on my clothes and the jacket from the smallest of the guys, ambling down the corridor, out into the dark night.

36

I walked flat mouthed along the quiet street, only vaguely aware of my location and for once scarcely taking any notice as one foot followed the other. My shadow rose and fell with each light above.

I just walked.

A lie.

I thought about how I could find ice cream and a comfy sofa with a TV.

Wasn't that what you're supposed to do when your heart breaks?

I stopped walking, my head reeling as the thoughts bubbled to the surface. Heart-broken. Not me.

I barely summoned up the energy for the extra breath to allow the deep sigh.

I watched a bus roll past; watched it stop a few car lengths away. I should get on the bus, I knew. I should get on and never look back.

A young woman stepped to the pavement and I stared after, my thoughts turning to those who'd stepped from those coaches and assigned themselves to the foul torture of that place.

I thought of the waving hands and smiling faces at the windows; the small children sat next to caring parents who had no idea what would happen.

I imagined their heartache as they realised. If they could still feel at all now. It would be more than I felt, but it put my pain in context.

I was alive and well. I'd get over her loss. Her betrayal. Eventually, I told myself.

The bus pulled away and I saw the neon sign for a twenty-four-hour internet cafe. I needed to let them know, at least. I needed to let them call in the rescue team. I needed to let them call in the army, the police or whoever would come and save the day.

The cafe was empty and I could barely raise my arm to

pay for the minimum hour.

I tapped in the numbers for the IP address from memory and then my sixteen-digit credentials flowed through to the screen in a blur of my fingers.

I waited the five minutes I knew it would take, then I checked all around me. With the place still empty, I typed.

Half an hour passed before the message completed, sending everything they needed to know. Everything. And things I shouldn't have said.

A reply came back after barely a pause.

Instructions:

1) Detain FB (Alive). Seize project data. Eliminate project hierarchy.

2) Call local law enforcement when objective complete.

The instructions had no ambiguity.

I knew what it meant for me. I knew what it meant for her. For all of them.

But I couldn't do it. I typed a reply.

I told them I wasn't able to complete the mission. I told them I wasn't capable. I told them I didn't have the equipment. I told them I was broken and cried, tears falling to the keyboard.

I sniffed and wiped my eyes with the back of my hands, but the tears kept coming. I cried for what seemed like forever, looking up only as I heard a cough at my side.

I was about to complain for privacy when I saw the guy holding out a box of tissues, beaming with a warm smile.

"Are you okay, ma'am?" he said.

"No," I replied, taking a tissue. "But I will be," I said and thanked him as I wiped my face and blew my nose.

I took a deep breath and deleted my reply, replacing it with a single word.

Acknowledged.

37

Leaving the Berettas had been a mistake. I understood that now.

I'd let the emotion cloud my judgement, but not anymore.

With the sun rising at my back I found myself in the bad part of town, trying not to remember the last time I'd been here as my knuckles knocked at the door, both its panes still boarded.

After what seemed like an age, I heard movement from the other side and I prepared myself. The door opened a crack and before the chain went taut I charged ahead, pushing the full trash can in front.

The momentum snapped the loose metal from its mooring and I followed through with my hands gripping the thin handles. The guy fell to the floor after two involuntary back-steps, his weapon dropping no sooner than I'd expected.

I threw the can over the man laying supine, his hands and legs struggling to gain traction in the air like a tortoise stranded on its shell. I scooped up his battered baseball bat and pushed the business end to his throat.

"Where do you get your shit from?" I said.

He calmed, quietening his struggle as I spoke.

After two more polite requests and the shattering of his left knee, he let the information go.

I smashed the other to keep him still, then deconstructed his two mobiles and the landline into tiny plastic pieces before I headed off down the street, swinging the bat in my hand with a new-found enthusiasm for my work.

Five streets over, the houses improved a hundred-fold; the area clean, a better class of living for higher up the chain.

The address he'd given had an intact front door and I circled to an alley between the backs of the houses and found the target by counting along the row. I pulled myself over the fence and knew myself to be lucky as I found the back door wide open.

Creeping up to the windows looking out to the garden, I fixed on a young man watching TV, the side of his torso and the lower part of his body at least; the rest obscured by the straight-back chair.

I made a mental note. He was an early riser. I'd have to go hard and fast, both because he might be high, his pain threshold raised and the Ruger KP90 on the arm of his chair.

I counted six cans of beer and bottles, pizza boxes with the flaps open, single slices uneaten.

I saw more signs of a high occupancy; ashtrays overflowing with stubs, crack pipes strewn across a coffee table. Either that or they were signs he was a lazy fuck.

Creeping in through the open door, I stepped with care across the hallway as I acquainted myself with the interior layout, soon figuring he'd see me when I crossed into the room; another reason to go in all guns blazing, metaphorically, as I didn't yet have one.

Running my hand along the length of the ash, it would have to do.

With the bat primed above my head, I charged into the room, bounding forward with the bat swinging in an arc, smashing into his ribs to push the air in near silence from his lungs. The Ruger, with its stainless-steel slide, remained on the arm of the chair as his hands went to his chest and the bat swung out again only to return to his head.

He'd be dead if I hadn't pulled the final swing.

Instead he was out cold. He was a bad man, but more punishment than was necessary sat outside my remit.

I checked the pistol, tutting as I flicked the safety on. Pulling back the slide I saw one in the chamber, the magazine filled to burst with fourteen forty-fives. It looked as if someone had fired it many times before and it needed a serious clean after being shoved into a thousand pockets, lint covering the inside of the chamber and the rounds.

I pushed the gun inside my suit jacket; I had no time to check in any more detail and toured the ground floor, swinging the bat to find all bare of anything useful.

I took the stairs, finding all three rooms above were empty, except for the great bags of weed and a table dusted with white powder. I tried not to breathe in as I let the door shut.

I found no tools, which meant I'd have to pay a little trip to a familiar address first.

After leaving the house with my primary aim fulfilled, I took from him one last thing; a distinctive set of keys which led me to a mode of transport I wasn't expecting, but then again, I'd always thought of the Dodge Viper as a drug dealer's car.

I didn't waste any time and I let the tyres eat up the road, ripping through the tarmac mile after mile until I was back at the little estate I'd already stopped considering as my home.

Leaving the car parked someway down the road and out of sight, I was back at fifty-four. Only Brad was around, the others still in bed, if the parked cars were anything to go by.

I could see him pottering at the far edge of the garden, cutting back the already short grass as it met the fence. I was in and out within a few moments, changed to trainers, jeans and a more discrete top; anything was more conservative than what I'd been wearing.

Finally swapping the oversized jacket for a bomber to better conceal the Ruger, the final items collected were my thin leather gloves, which I'd brought with me just for this time.

There was nothing else in this house I wasn't happy to say goodbye to and I was through next door's gate and turning the key in the back door in barely a moment.

I found Lenara sitting in her dressing gown in the living room, the TV on low. She seemed troubled, not looking up from the ice pack she held at her hand.

"You can't feel the pain, can you?" I said as I ambled closer.

"No. Sit down," she said, still not meeting my eye.

"Since the injury."

"What happened?" I said as I sat on an armchair next to her.

"Car accident. A long time ago now."

"Frank's still trying to find you a cure," I said, but it wasn't a question.

"He's close. He's devoted his life."

"Why?" I said, shuffling forward to the edge of the chair.

"We fell in love. What else is there?"

"I'm sorry, but he doesn't love you," I said.

Her head snapped up for the first time. "Just because he's fucking Alarica?" she said, her voice still calm.

I paused, holding back my reply for a moment. "Yes. I'm sorry."

"And you, too, if he had the chance," she replied.

"But I haven't. I won't," I said, shaking my head.

She gave a shallow nod and turned back to the ice.

"He has needs I can't satisfy, but when he's fixed me, she's gone from our lives and I'll forgive him. In the meantime, I need him, want him to be happy," she replied. "And then she's gone," she added, before I could say anything more.

"Do you know how he's finding his cure?"

"My cure," she said and shook her head. "I'm not the doctor."

Is she just burying her head in the sand? I asked myself.

"I'm just going to go upstairs. I think I dropped something in the spare room. Do you mind?"

"Go ahead," she said, nodding towards the door.

I took one last look at her, then taking each step with care, I headed upstairs.

The room was the same as I'd left it, although the contents of the desk had been cleared away and the code had changed on the door.

I tried another, my name this time, then turned down the stairs, my hands in my pockets as I stared at the gun pointed up towards me.

38

"He's a good man," Lenara said from the bottom of the stairs, the Bersa Thunder .380 clamped too tight in her right hand.

"Then he's a good man doing terrible things," I said, swinging slowly to the right.

"He's doing this for me," she said, with the small gun tracking my movement.

"Why?" I swung to the left, letting the speed build.

"He loves me," she replied, moving her hand with my sway.

"He was driving the car," I said. "Wasn't he?"

She nodded.

"But he doesn't drive," I replied.

"Not a day since. I told you, he loves me and he will make this right. I can't let you get in the way. I can't let you stop him."

"What makes you think I can?" I replied, the swing building this way and that.

"I've seen it in your eyes, from the beginning. There's something about you," she said, the gun tracking my pendulum movement.

"Then you'll understand I've got to try," I replied. My movement stopped, my shoulders pushing in the opposite direction but her hand continued to sweep away.

I pulled the gun from my pocket, flicking the safety off. The round bounced off the front door's toughened glass, blood and brain matter following behind.

At least she didn't feel it, I thought. One member of the hierarchy crossed off the list.

I jumped down the stairs five at a time, taking the gun and checked the contents of the magazine, counting in a flash the eight rounds and one in the chamber. As sunlight streamed from the other side of the front door, the deep reds staining the glass brought back memories of family trips to church.

Back at fifty-four, the garden at least, I searched for

Brad but I couldn't see him anywhere, despite the shed door standing open.

After struggling through the mounds of clutter, I found the bolt croppers behind an old lawn mower crusted with long-dried grass.

When the wooden floor creaked, I turned to see Brad stood blocking out most of the light and I heard his voice for the first time.

"Can I help?" he said, beaming a wide smile with his stare fixed on the croppers and his eyebrows raised.

"No thanks. Got to go," I said, moving past him and pocketing a pair of pliers found on the side as I did.

Without looking back, I was up into my old bedroom one last time. Glancing out of the window, I could see no commotion next door. No police cars squealed to a stop, and I knew they never would; not as long as Frank was still in charge. Until I called them, of course.

Pulling the magazine from the Ruger, I used the pliers on the first round. After quickly finishing the modification, I slid it back into the butt of the gun, before jabbing it in the corner of my jacket pocket.

Jogging through the woods, I arrived sooner than I'd expected at the weathered concrete still rising from the forest floor. I wasn't sure why I thought it would no longer be there.

Walking up to the concrete structure, I looked down past the rusted iron bars. I saw what I'd seen the last time, but this was my first proper look.

Lining up the jaws of the croppers with the dulled chrome lock, I pulled up, twisting around to fix on a sound close by from the forest. An early morning dog walker perhaps, even though it would be the first time.

"It's only me," said Lenart's voice; not the last man I'd expected. I was ready for most things.

Resting the croppers to the head of the drain, he walked between the trees and into the clearing with his palms out at his front.

I left both guns in my pockets.

"You're with the Bureau, aren't you?" I said. An educated guess.

He nodded and let his hands drop. "You have me at an advantage?" he replied, his manner so different to what I'd ever seen.

"Specialist. International," I said. "You wouldn't know even if I told you."

"You know about Frank then?" he said.

I nodded. "How long have you known?" I replied, wary of any movement.

He didn't move. His feet stayed planted to the spot. "He's been under surveillance for a year now," he replied.

"Just you?"

"Just me."

"Celina? The kids?" I said.

"It's complicated. They know nothing," he said with his voice staying calm.

"What do you know?" I replied, pointing my head down the drain as I followed his gaze to the croppers.

"Bad things," he said. "What's your plan?"

"I have orders," I said. "I'm closing the place down."

"I didn't hear that," he said.

"They will be told. After," I replied.

"Okay, I get that. I've been asking for a task force to take this place out for a long while now. When does it arrive?" he said, looking around the forest, maybe half expecting armed police to jump out from the treeline.

"I am the task force."

"A one-woman army."

"Something like that," I said. "And now you," I added. "You carrying?"

He shook his head.

I pulled the croppers from their rest and the lock pinged off, the bulk of the metal falling with a thud to the base of the ring.

He came to the other side of the concrete and helped me pull up the grill, letting it come to rest after its hinged edge shrieked with each degree it turned.

Looking back, I watched as Lenart held his hand out to steady me, but I put up my palm to decline as I rested my right foot on the first of the iron rungs fixed into the side.

Step after step I lowered myself down, glancing between the dark floor and Lenart's face smiling back.

"I'm sorry," he said.

"What for?" I replied, looking up as I came head level with the top of the forest floor.

"How I acted before," he replied, peering down past me. "Part of my cover."

"Okay, and I'm sorry for drugging you," I replied.

He looked back with his eyes widening.

"I thought that was Celina. Hah," he said, laughing as he shook his head.

"Can I ask you something?"

"Of course," he replied.

"Why were you so nice to me suddenly?"

He didn't reply straight away. "I don't know, or maybe I knew something wasn't right."

The reply made little sense, but I moved lower and caught a draft of air I could only just notice, my attention on the thin metal I felt with hands out in front and into the darkness. My fingers were working over a louvred grill, the type you get for ventilation and not on a drain.

"A ventilation shaft," I said out loud as the pieces came together in my mind. I felt around the edge for some catch or release lever.

Instead, I found four posi-drive screws that my fingers couldn't get a purchase on. I looked up as I stood, half surprised to see Lenart staring back at me.

"Can't get through. Need more tools," I said.

He peered down, his eyes pinched as I rattled up the rungs of the ladder and out into the open before he could barely move out of the way.

"You wait here. Protect this position."

"What with?" he replied, lowering his brow as he

looked around.

I hesitated, then chucked the Ruger to his feet. He pulled it from the grass, checked the chamber, the safety and the magazine just as I had done. He had some level of professionalism.

"It needs a clean," he said.

I nodded.

"Does it fire?" he said, and I nodded again, giving him little chance to pose any more questions before I ran at full speed to the house.

Still no one was up. Brad nowhere, at least not in the garden or in the shed. With the screwdriver in my back pocket, I headed through the house, racking my brains for where I'd seen a torch before.

Glancing at the computer, I moved the mouse and the screen lit. I typed in the IP address and tapped out a message.

You could have warned me about the friendlies.

I turned.

Lenart came through the door, his breathing heavy.

The computer chimed to signify a reply. I turned back to the screen and closed the browser with a click, turning straight towards the door and the gun pointing in my direction.

No friendlies.

39

"That explains a lot," I said standing to my full height.

"Explains what?" he replied, his eyes tightening to a squint as he let the door close at his back.

"I almost had you figured out."

"How so?" he replied

"Your office in town doesn't know who you are," I said, watching the twitch of his eyelids. "Your car doesn't have enough mileage." His eyebrows almost jumped this time.

"Huh."

I could only just hear his reply.

"You only do enough miles to go around the corner to the factory each day," I said, fixing him with my stare as he smiled.

"You scheming little bitch," he replied. "It hasn't done you any good though, has it?"

I shrugged. "You're not Bureau then?" I replied, moving my left foot forward a step.

"Oh, I am. Stand still," he said, his voice back to the flat tone I'd known for the last few weeks. "At least that's one of my jobs."

I nodded with a grin rising.

"Why the fuck are you smiling?" he said as I sensed the anger building.

"Now I understand why I've been sent here. We couldn't trust the Bureau to get the job done. They know about you."

His eyes flared wide, but soon returned to a squint. "I know what you're trying to do, but it won't work."

"I'm proof, aren't I?" I replied, my grin getting wider. "Ally had you figured out. I take it she didn't know. She almost gave you up without realising you were working for Frank. Nosey old pervert was what she called you, I think."

He smiled in reply and I could guess he wasn't thinking about his job.

"Smart kid, but not smart enough. I didn't figure you

out," he said, continuing as I didn't reply. "Only Frank knew what I was doing. We had a chat and formed a pact. I would be an observation post from the outside."

"And protect him from the Bureau. In return for what? Money?"

He nodded. "And a few other perks."

I felt the bile rise in my stomach and he smiled at my reaction.

"And you started being nice to me because Frank had a word."

"Maybe," he replied. "Anyway, this arrangement was never going to be forever. He just needed a few more weeks."

I turned to see Brad coming through the kitchen door, his face missing all the shock and surprise that should be there when you walk into a room and see someone holding a gun.

"You, too," I said, remembering the screwdriver still in my back pocket.

"I'm afraid so," he said. "We all have our own interests to look after."

"And your part, Brad?" I said, switching my look between the two.

"He watched when I couldn't be here. It had to look like I went to work each day," Lenart said.

I nodded. "But instead you went to the factory."

He shrugged.

"And Celina?" I added, preparing myself for anything he might say.

He laughed. "She had a role."

"More continuous coverage?" I replied.

"No, hers was a little more specific," Lenart said.

It was Brad who filled the silence that followed.

"She was here to keep him happy."

Lenart laughed again. "A perk."

"Are you married?" I replied, the words slipping from my mouth.

"God no," he said, moving back in disgust.

"Why would she?" I replied, mirroring his twisted

expression. I watched him look down at himself and smile. He looked up, his right eyebrow raised and lowered.

"We have something over her," Lenart said, going back to the squint.

I nodded, inside feeling like I should grab the screwdriver and plunge it into his crotch. Somehow I managed to keep my voice level as I spoke. "Makes more sense," I said, forcing a laugh. "The kids?" I replied.

"Look, this isn't confession time. Yeah, they're mine. She had to look after them, too. Enough questions," he said, raising his voice.

"And still you brought me in?" I replied.

"I'm not a monster. I wanted her to enjoy her life too. Enough."

"I hope you both know that your involvement is just as bad as what Frank's doing down there," I said, turning to nod in the general direction of the factory.

Lenart shrugged and I guessed Brad was doing the same. I didn't have a chance to do much else as I glanced to the sound of footsteps at the top of the stairs.

Celina.

Lenart looked her way and I heard the moment she saw the gun; the moment the breath pulled from her lungs.

"What's going on down here?"

"Go back upstairs," Lenart said as she came further down, looking wide eyed with her head snapping between me and the gun pointed in my direction.

"What the hell are you doing?" she said. "Brad, what's going on?"

Brad shrugged his shoulders.

"Go back up or you could get hurt," Lenart said.

Celina continued to flow down the stairs.

"Celina," he added, his voice growing more urgent.

"What's she done? Where the hell did you get a gun?" she said, almost at the bottom step.

"You won't understand." His gaze was back on me when he spoke.

I took my chance to speak.

"Did you know he works for the government?"

"Did," she replied.

"Still is," I said.

"Shut the fuck up, bitch," Lenart blurted.

"Lenart," Celina shouted back, and I spoke again.

"He still is, but he's double crossed them and now he's on the wrong side of the law in a huge way."

"What's this all about, Lenart? Why is she saying that?" Celina said, moving closer to him.

Lenart spun the gun around and Celina stopped in her tracks. His face grew as alarmed as hers and he went to bring the gun back to bear on me.

I didn't wait, my hand grabbing the screwdriver from my back pocket and I threw it, letting go of the long metal shaft before the gun could arc through the curve.

His hands reacted to the pain in his chest before his brain had time to process the new object embedded there. I heard the dull thud of the striker hitting the bullet I'd used the pliers on to empty of smokeless powder.

Celina leapt for the gun as it fell from his hand, catching it before it hit the floor.

Lenart fell to his knees, his back angled downwards trying to look at the orange handled driver poking from his chest with his hands moving towards the foreign object.

I turned, ducking as I saw Brad's arm swing in my direction. The Ruger clicked, useless in Celina's hands.

I rose, springing up, launching a double-fisted push up through his jaw to smash his mouth shut.

Dazed, he swung wide, clipping me on the shoulder, but the blow still had enough force to send me to the ground. I watched as he stumbled toward me, pausing only as a vase came out of nowhere and shattered at his temple.

The round exploded from the Bersa in the time the smashing pottery had given me to pull it free from my pocket.

He was down and wasn't getting up. Hierarchy or just self-defence, I wasn't sure which.

I turned, the Ruger out in both of Celina's hands pointed at Brad.

She turned as I did. With it the Ruger came in my direction.

Not her too?

Ignoring the gun, I looked instead at Lenart.

Celina's glassy-eyed gaze followed, as did the gun.

I stepped to her side and she let me take it. I ejected the dead round and pushed it back into my pocket.

Celina couldn't take her eyes from Lenart's face, drained and pale as he lay on the floor with his eyes wide.

"You need to get out of here. Take the children and go."

"They're at a friend's house. What the hell's going on? You. Him. Brad? I don't get it. None of you are who I thought you were," she said, for the first time looking towards me.

"I am who you thought I was, but I'm not an au pair. I work for an organisation connected to your government. I'm here to find a terrible man and bring him to justice."

"Lenart?" she said, her voice rising.

"No. Frank Bukia, but Lenart and Brad were working for him."

She held her breath, then stumbled with words that wouldn't come out. "What... What is Frank doing that's so bad?"

"I won't tell you and I never want you to find out, but you must trust me." I paused.

She didn't move, giving no indication of what she might do.

"I'm one of the good guys and if I succeed, the good guys will win."

She was silent as Lenart gurgled his last breath.

"Why should I trust you?"

"You don't have to. I wouldn't in your situation. All you have to do is get the kids and yourself away from this place and do it as fast as you can."

"I want to call the police."

"You won't be able to. Not yet. They won't respond."

"What have you done?"

"Not me. Frank has them all sewn up. He wants to handle everything his own way. I've got to go, I'm afraid, and I don't think I'll ever see you again."

She stepped forward as I moved towards her and leant in for a hug. She didn't hesitate.

"There's something I need to tell you," she said. "The reason I'm here. The reason I've been with Lenart all this time." Her voice sang in my ear.

I pulled back, holding the tops of her shoulders and looked her in the eye.

"I don't want to know. You're free now," I said, and she pulled me tight to her chest.

As we separated, she turned her head and planted her lips on mine. We held there for a long time.

"Go," I said. "You won't want to see this," and bent down to pull the screwdriver from Lenart's torso.

40

Back at the ventilation shaft within ten minutes, I threw the croppers into the tree line and the loose screws to the dirt floor of the shaft. The stainless-steel grill followed the croppers like a frisbee; then, after it went three different layers of cardboard-edged filters.

Inside the tunnel darkness filled the space. But what else had I expected? I'd been distracted from the search for the torch.

The push of air had grown stronger and filled with a fast, metallic whine as it sent my hair backwards. Curling into the tunnel by angling my shoulders, I closed my eyes to keep away the dust I unsettled. As I pushed forward, holding the screwdriver out at my front, it led the way, probing the concrete, sweeping left and right.

When it felt like I'd shuffled a good distance, but with no view or change to the ground at my knees, I could only tell my progress as the screwdriver touched something solid ahead, before slipping to the side and jumping forward to alarm against what I guessed to be spinning metal fan blades.

Pulling back to let the echo die and whilst keeping hold of the screwdriver, I crept my hands forward along the edge of the curved wall until I touched at the cold metal.

My fingers crept towards the centre and soon found another wire mesh grill barring the way.

With most of my caution abandoned, I felt all around the edge of the grill, setting the screwdriver on each of the four screws holding it in place, but I still had to figure out some way of stopping the fan.

Before I released the last two screws, I backed out; squinting at the brightness outside, I scrabbled around in the undergrowth to find the croppers from where I'd thrown them.

I had the grill off and at my back within a moment. Covering my face with my upper arm, I launched the heavy croppers forward, their bulk crashing against the thin metal.

The push of the wind dropped, but took up a heartbeat later.

With great care, my fingertips moved as close to the whine as I dared, but try as I might I couldn't find the croppers.

Backing out of the tunnel again, I moved to the entrance to let the light penetrate so I could figure out my next move. The little amount of light coming past showed me the croppers had been spat out and lay on the other side of the blades, out of reach for another attempt.

A thought of shooting at the blades flashed into my head. Then came the sight of my dead body, killed by flying shrapnel.

Instead, back out of the shaft, I found the widest and thickest log from the undergrowth, but had to return to the surface to find one small enough to manoeuvre into the tight space.

Shuffling my feet along the shaft, I pushed the log out in front, moving to sit when I drew close to the blades. Pushing with my feet, the log attacked the blade in a shower of splinters, peppering around me as the fan ground to a sudden stop, groaning as it fought against the wood.

Spitting out wooden needles, I edged forward and with a small click echoing through the tunnel, the fan ceased its complaint.

Feeling around at the stopped blades, their surface jagged and bent from the assault, I had to pull the log away to give myself enough room and slid the remains of the ragged wood behind me.

With my hands out in the centre of the tunnel, I found where the blades met in the middle. Working to the outside, I felt one of the misshapen blades before moving my hands to the side as I searched for the next one.

The space between the metal was still nowhere near wide enough for me to squeeze between and I grabbed the blade with both hands and pulled it towards me, but it hardly moved.

I tried again, this time pushing at the metal, then leant

back and repeated with my feet. It still didn't move enough.

I remembered the heavy croppers the other side.

Being careful not to scrape my arm with the rough edge of the metal, I managed to slide through up to my shoulders and the tips of my fingers found the tool. With purchase between two fingers I pulled back, finding more grip with each movement.

A click echoed along the tunnel, coming from somewhere close to my right. Instinct had my grip releasing and I yanked my arm from between the blades just as they moved and were back to full speed before I'd taken a full breath, attacking the air with their newfound shape.

I let myself settle for a moment before grabbing the log at my back and turning away from the shower of splinters as the blades ground to a halt once more.

This time I waited, checking for the click to repeat whilst counting in my head and just able to retrieve the croppers with the long stretch of wood still in place. The safety cut-out control would give me thirty seconds or thereabouts before the metal would start the rotation again.

After ten seconds with the blades not moving, the system would trip, waiting for an automatic restart.

Leaving the log in place, I fumbled with the croppers to nip at the base of the metal before it tried to restart.

After two more rounds I had two blades snipped free and at my back out of the way. Now I could fit through.

Pushing the croppers back through the hole, I didn't want to repeat what I was about to attempt; I let the system click out and yanked the log, pushing it to my back, the numbers counting up in my head. I grabbed the remaining blades at high level and catapulted myself forward, swinging through the space I'd made.

My right foot hit the croppers against the wall, sending a jolt of pain up through my hip. My left hit something solid and I only just had my hips through the gap. The realisation hit me that the space after the fan was just short of my leg length. With fifteen seconds left, I bent my knees and crammed myself further in. With my torso in, bunched in the space, it only left my head between the last of the blades ten seconds before the shredded edge of the fan would whip around to grind at my neck.

Fumbling with my lower body, twisting this way and that, kicking at the solid walls, I had five seconds.

It was time to give up. I'd have to pull out and take more time to think. But no, that time had passed long ago.

With one last swing of my legs I twisted and finding no resistance, my legs were in a gap.

The relay echoed. I let go of the blades and with one last push I forced myself to the space I'd just found and had to hope it was big enough to save me.

41

There was enough room, but only just and now I'd stuffed myself in the space laying on my side with my hair dragging towards the spinning fan, strands pinging from my scalp. Pushing my hand to the wall, I squeezed a little further away to stop the pull of my hair.

Now only able to move my feet and bend a little at the knee, I probed out with the soles, tapping and listening to their hollow report. Pulling my feet up towards my ass as far as I could, I kicked out with all my might.

Bright light flooded the tight chamber as something released to the sound of metal clattering against a hard surface, echoing as my eyes squeezed shut to leave my legs hovering in free space.

I twisted to my front, letting my legs down at the waist, but found no solid purchase. I shuffled further over the edge, pausing only for a moment as I tried and failed to guess my bearings.

With little other choice, I dropped, bending my knees as I landed and stood squinting in a harsh white light.

Forcing my eyes as wide as I could, I found myself in the tunnel I'd looked along a few days before. I stood alone.

Taking a moment to enjoy the freedom from the claustrophobic bounds, I scanned along the bright magnolia tunnel.

The view was so different from when I'd glanced down from the room to my far left. I could just make out the glass doors in the distance. To my right were another set of doors within a minute's walk, behind which I saw none of the detail of the room I'd stood in at the other end. A faint sound of voices echoed towards me.

Collecting up the white grill I'd kicked out, I did my best to bend it back into shape and followed up the dust-covered wall, pushing it back in place. It looked only half right, but I guessed in a few minutes its appearance would no longer matter.

I turned down the long corridor to my left, squinting to the doors in the distance and thought about running towards them to take in the CCTV monitors and get a better feel for the layout.

I turned and ran in the opposite direction. For now, I still had surprise as my advantage.

I raced forward, light on my feet to the sound of the voices growing in volume and clarity, soon able to hear more than one person; those over-the-top commentators again.

Without a sound, the frosted glass door at the end of the corridor slid open with my pull at the handle, but the volume of the hurried talk would have masked all but a gunshot.

Following around the corner with a slow, cautious step, I kept my back to the wall with the Bersa in my right hand, soon bringing it to bear on the guy in the sharp suit. His jacket was two sizes larger than needed as he sat at a chair in front of a small desk with a compact television on top. The television blared with a cheering crowd giving a break from the two guys and their loud calls.

Behind him stood a door I guessed he should have been protecting.

As I came around the corner, he glanced up as if annoyed at the distraction, then double-took in my direction, his eyes going wide as if he knew I should be dead already.

His reactions were hair-trigger quick, but he made the wrong choice to underestimate my skill; his left-hand slapped at a panic button before I could stop him, tones already ringing out before my bullet smashed through his skull.

He should have gone for the gun first; instead, his hand dropped before it could reach the Glock 17 on the desk.

I paused for no longer than a second on the black composite. A generation three.

Self-defence, I said, but my voice disappeared into the ring of the alarm as I shouldered the door wide enough to get through.

Running along the short corridor on the other side, I

soon came to its end to find the doors still unlocked and I wondered at the purpose of the panic button.

Dismissing my question, I pushed through, half expecting to see a stream of workers walking from their rooms or finishing their tasks whilst laying whatever tools they had to the side and heading away from their stations.

There was nothing orderly about what I saw.

The view told me the panic button was the last resort. The ringing tones only called for real trouble and they should run from this place and abandon to the hills.

In a bright corridor with glass walls either side, I saw the vast rooms I'd glared at on the CCTV monitors. Trolley after trolley sat loaded with people. If they were asleep or unconscious I didn't know as they were unmoving, their skin gaunt in the dim glow. A rhythm of monitors sat at each side with a faint line tracing a heartbeat, twin blood pressure digits and other vital signs. They were at least alive.

Towards the end of the room, metal clattered to the floor, small instruments pinging to the polished concrete with white coats running to exits in the distance; their screams heard above the two tone as they jostled their way through the bottleneck.

No matter what monstrous act they'd just been committing, I'd have to leave them be. Unless they had a gun pointed in my direction, or in their hand, or wore a suit or a badge or a decrying look that marked them out as high on the organisation chart.

A shot rang off the glass wall at my side and I replied with my loud response dead ahead to doors which had just opened.

Two shots more and a suit fell to the floor, leaving the door to swing open at his back and expose the two more taking cover at the frame.

I reeled off another two shots in their direction. They ignored my fair warning, leaping forward to die soon after.

I flashed the gun left and right, down to four .380s in the Bersa. I promised myself single shots from now on.

Gritting my teeth at the waste of the rounds, I fired once, twice, three times at the glass a few panels down before it shattered. With one more shot to my right, I discarded the spent Bersa, then finished up the job with one from the Glock.

Jumping through the first gap I'd made and bending low to keep my head and back below the level of the trolleys, I shuffled forward, trying to avoid the debris abandoned in the panic.

I was three or four trolleys away from the glass corridor before I went to my knees and dared a look back.

Seeing three guys had appeared in oversized suit jackets, with their heads swivelling either side, I ducked back down when I watched them moving off in different directions whilst one stayed in the corridor.

I shuffled forward to put as much space between me and the guy hunting me down.

With my head low, I searched for the exit in the vast room, knowing only the rough direction from a hurried glance. As I crawled, I had to force myself to keep focus, to stop staring at the faces and trying to turn off the recognition as face after face alarmed my internal database. I couldn't stop myself from looking at the faces of those who I'd glimpsed on one of the many coaches, or walking to and from the diner.

I couldn't help but pause as I recognised the motionless form of the boy who'd waved from a coach as the driver stopped to offer help. His gaunt, pallid face still showed the faint lines on his forehead where the head brace had once been. Close up, most looked like they were asleep, but others seemed in a painful restless trance. Each seemed to have a body part missing; limbs no longer there. Stumps ringed with red-raw stitches, or blood-soaked bandages.

I forced myself to move on, fighting to keep silent but soon realising I'd lost track of the guy who'd been following. Only the occasional clatter of metal gave me any hint of how close he was getting.

My view cleared between several trolleys. I was just a short sprint through empty space from the double doors which had been the scene of the hurried mass-escape only moments before.

Glancing back, I jumped from my crouch with the Glock pointed out and aimed in anticipation.

My assailant had the same stance and saw me rise, ready with a reaction. Both of us corrected our aims and two rounds rang off at the same time. Each was a good shot, but I had less work to do. I'd known in the moment I would fire; his had been a reaction.

He went down, the round smashing into his shoulder.

He'd had a good aim; a little to the right and we would both have been on the floor clutching at a hole that shouldn't be there.

The thoughts didn't have time to linger. Our exchange had alerted the remaining two and I could see through the glass they were changing direction, following the sounds and would soon be ready to half the odds, thinking they would still win.

I hurried through the double doors and found some sort of anti-room with another door opposite. Strong disinfectant hung thick in the air. Stainless steel counters lined up either side, above which glass-fronted cabinets rested to the walls, each full of white boxes with markings that looked medical and names I thought I could unscramble if I paid any attention.

Without lingering I was through the double set of doors and into another place I'd seen on the CCTV; an operating theatre, thankful the table stood empty.

I carried on through to the other side, but I didn't continue out of the room. Instead I headed to the far-right corner and waited with the borrowed Glock pointed at the noise I'd heard at my back.

A moment later, the double doors swung wide. I shot with no hesitation.

Two shots rang off from the Glock, replied by two in return, but their blind firing did little else than dent the counters. Mine took one of them to the floor, jamming the door wide and giving me a perfect line of sight for his companion in the last few moments of his life.

I scolded myself at my lack of will power, checking the remaining rounds as I crossed the theatre to the bodies.

Twelve discharges from the Glock. Fourteen left in the Ruger.

Stooping over the nearest, my feet on the edge of a thick soup of crimson and other liquids I didn't want to think of, I hesitated as I heard the rattling of trolleys beyond the door.

My pause passed and I pulled the warm Glock from his limp hand, slipped the magazine from the grip and let the rest drop, leaping away from the splash.

Turning back and through the single door, I continued my journey into another corridor with the same glass lining the walls as before. However, this glass was dark and gave the impression of thick concrete either side.

The corridor ended and I listened at its steel door, giving a twist to the long handle before nudging it to open to a crack. With no sound warning me from the other side and with a virtual cacophony of danger from where I'd just come, I let the door swing open.

A set of concrete steps stood in the centre of a wide foyer, the stairs rising as they circled.

Doors to my right seemed to head back to the warehouse of unwitting guests. Beside those doors was another single door, and I had to conclude it was the other theatre I'd seen on the screen. The one I'd caught sight of the gruesome operation.

In front of me were two more steel doors, banding with steel plate riveted across its surface. Another sat to its right. I had no idea what these rooms could hold, but both were important enough to be buried in this secret underground complex.

42

Stepping out into the foyer with the activity beyond the door at my back growing louder, I checked the Glock whilst running from the door to the concrete of the stairs as a shield for my back. I couldn't help but wonder if my pursuers would be foolish enough to burst out from the corridor.

Whilst I'd run, I noted the doors as I passed. Both were secured with swipe card locks, but I'd seen no one wearing ID passes.

I waited, unable to hear their chase now the steel door had sealed. The only sounds I could catch were from above. The long blast of a car horn. A second with a short burst in reply. Then an orchestra of horns of all tones, but each ending with a dull crash and grind of metal.

The noise above was soon in the distant past, their intrusion forgotten as my attention snapped to the heavy metal door and the face peering out, the legs sliding past the safety of the barrier. A Glock pointed out from the crack of the door to a place where I wasn't. Another joined at his side.

I almost felt sorry as I ended their lives, but I had no time to take careful aim and disable their arms from holding the killing machines, or their legs from running to safety and fighting another day. Instead, I did them a favour; I saved them from the trauma of crippling pain and years of incarceration, if they'd been lucky.

As the echoes died to silence, I heard nothing from above. Nothing from behind where the two dead guys lay.

Pulling out from behind the safety of the stairwell, I padded over to their bodies, taking a moment to rifle their pockets whilst trying not to settle on their faces. I didn't need to see who they'd been.

The eerie quiet continued as I searched and found what I hoped for. Taking the unmarked white plastic key cards from their back pockets, I stepped away from the blood before the growing pool reached my feet.

Neither card worked on the first door, but the second

opened on the first try. Humming fans and a wash of cooled air greeted me as I pulled the door wide, where I saw a blanket of blinking LEDs.

Flicking on the light switch, I ticked off an objective as I scanned the fronts of the servers, but before I could congratulate myself too much, my survey caught on a monitor to the side and a brace of CCTV images.

After scanning each of the sixteen views across the screen, I turned back to the large computers. On finding the small book-sized tapes, I held my fingers to each of the power buttons. With the newfound quietness of the room, I ran my fingers along the front of the computers, unlatching each of the front-loading drives.

With the drives piled at my feet, I turned back to the door and searched around the room for something to carry the load in. All I could find was the metal bin, and I loaded drives and the back-up tapes to fill to the top.

Turning back to the matrix of images, I lingered to get my bearings. In the top left corner, four images showed what I guessed to be the outside of the factory, which I soon confirmed when in the last of the four I saw the base of the giant chimney visible for miles around.

In each of those four images, the roads filled with grid-locked traffic. Cars edged forward in short angry movements, but all in a common direction. I followed the flow, not helped by the cameras looking in different directions, but after a moment and a short leap of logic, I reassured myself they were all running towards the exit gates.

In one screen I watched a disturbance. Smoke rose from a car blocking the road. People were jumping out of their vehicles to point and shout, then gathered to push the wreck to the side of the road.

Only a wide tanker lorry battled against the flow, reversing from the opposite direction to head towards the base of the chimney. I couldn't help but imagine what sort of monster, or massive force, they thought had come to their place of work that meant they had to be in such a hurry.

They were running from me. They were running from their reckoning, but if there were any good people amongst them, it would be themselves they would have to run from before long.

Scanning across the images, I hoped Frank would be the last to leave, but I guessed that like a rat, he would have been the first, no doubt with a helicopter on standby for just this eventuality.

I scanned the pictures of empty laboratories and offices with equipment strewn to the floor. Desks where monitors shined with their last work. Spreadsheets. Photos of patients. Lines of text, each with a message window complaining I'd killed their network.

Moving to the next image I came to the vacant operating theatre, then its twin and my worst fear. In the colour image I could make out the blood-red floor and the gaunt, white naked body missing a leg.

Squeezing my eyes closed for a moment, I hoped the guy had gone quickly, but flinched when I opened them to see his arm rise and fall on the screen.

They would pay. I'd make them.

My attention fell to a view of the scene at number fifty-six and the scarlet front door. The house still deserted. No cops. No paramedics.

Three figures moved across the next few screens. The first was a camera pointed at the two steel doors, one of which I was behind, with two people passing the other side. They were the pair I recognised from earlier, walking with a caution which told me they had no idea where I was.

The next screen faced opposite the other and showed another in their same suit uniform, but he soon left the view. Just as he disappeared out of sight, I caught the flash of his assault rifle's stock.

I checked the Glock, exchanging the nine-round magazine for a full seventeen and opened the door.

Bullets spat towards me, the blasts pounding against the metal just as I'd dived back, lucky that I hadn't crawled forward into the path of the next un-aimed shots.

Leaving the door wide, I'd dropped to the floor and twisted to the monitor to get a better view. Rather than taking in where they'd fired at me from, I saw Frank and Ally running around the rising steps; the guy with the assault rifle was nowhere to be seen.

The echo of the shots died back and I knew he waited in hope I'd emerge again and he wouldn't have to come and find me. His orders would be to wait, holding me back to give the pair the time to get away.

I ran the replay of his shots through my head, counting twice to make sure I'd got it right.

The first was an automatic burst, maybe six rounds. The second a clear group of three. I needed him to fire once more to confirm my thought.

Glancing to the CCTV, I saw the pair emerge in one of the offices, Frank in the lead and Ally close at his back with a handgun in her hand. Her survey was everywhere as the bright sun streamed through the windows.

I didn't have time to be pinned down and this guy knew it.

I took the first of the disks from the bin, sending it clattering through the opening to slap against the concrete, all whilst swapping my view to track the pair escaping. The throw had the desired effect and a three-shot burst replied to confirm what I'd thought.

Obvious now, despite the echo.

An M16 with eighteen rounds to go.

I threw another and took him down to fifteen, but he'd already wised up to my attempts and didn't loose off another volley as I released the third of the disks.

After upending the bin and stuffing the backup tapes into the bomber jacket pockets, I lay flat to the floor, throwing another disk, but this time in the opposite direction. Six shots burst out to follow.

With nine rounds left, I tried to make myself as flat to the floor as possible, trying not to think my luck would run out soon and a stray ricochet could get me any time he fired.

Lifting my hand, I fired in a direction I thought he could be, trading my three rounds for another six of his. Now was the time to test his metal; was he counting or was he an amateur? Did he have another magazine at the ready or a second weapon just for this circumstance?

I threw a disk and let another round off. I'd got my three, but could no longer afford to be flat.

As I heard the tell-tale solid click of the empty magazine, I leapt up through the opening and caught him in my sights, but at a very poor angle to the side of the staircase.

He stood alone with the new magazine in his hands.

My record to reload was three seconds, but I'd done it over hundreds of times on the range. He was less than I was and was still fumbling to eject the old magazine. His hands still played with the catch as his gaze fixed on me, settling to the darkness inside the barrel of my Glock.

His magazine fell to the floor as the lead flattened inside the back of his skull.

I didn't linger to untangle the weapon from his body. Instead, I raced up the concrete stairs with my feet echoing to arrive in a small glass lobby; a bubble of glass with a locked door to my front.

I pumped four rounds at the plate glass, smashing out the remains with the butt end of a fire extinguisher. But it was taking far too long to get through.

Eight rounds left; Nine in the spare and the Ruger, which I didn't know if it would fire again.

I ran through some industrial foyer, magnolia walls of concrete with daylight streaming in from either side. I recounted their journey, finding the cameras high in the corners of the ceiling so I could pinpoint the direction they'd taken and follow.

Running, I glanced outside. The traffic had gone, leaving just exhaust fumes breezing in through the windows and wisps of smoke rising from the wrecked car resting in the distant tree line, the tanker parked at the base of the giant chimney. The sinking ship had emptied of its rats, their prey left below to die.

I raced through an office, jumping over debris to the smell of hot coffee and the carpet marked with recent spills. Pushing open the door to a stairwell, I ignored the steps and carried on through the offices, guessing at their likely escape through the open doors the other end.

I ran through, searching left and right through the windows but there was nothing but a few abandoned cars left tight to the building.

But now my view was blocked by the concrete walls themselves. Turning around, I backtracked my journey, speeding over swivel chairs, around tall files spilt to the floor and climbed the steps I'd passed once already.

Up through the first floor, then the second and third, I burst open the doors at the summit, running onto the gravel-topped roof. Squinting to the beating sun, I tried to take in the full view.

I was in the middle of the roof. To my right I could see tall barriers raised at the main exit of the compound and the tall chimney marking my way, its black contents billowing out into the sky. With the horizon just a sea of trees, if they weren't going by road then I had no hope of finding them. If they were escaping by road, I could never catch them.

I ran towards the closest edge of the building, ninety degrees to the chimney. As I reached the concrete horizon, my view filled with the emptiness of the scene. All cars gone, the road littered with white coats and belongings no longer needed.

I carried on along the edge, jogging towards the chimney and watching as more of the same space opened up in front of me. Empty parking spaces. Debris to the ground. White coats. Briefcases, white access cards and papers strewn across the tarmac.

Then I caught the strong stench of gasoline and I half expected to see another car-wreck abandoned, but what I saw gave me more pause than I could afford.

43

A brick building wrapped around the base of the chimney and I watched as five figures rushed from a black Jeep with the doors pushed wide, hurrying to the entrance. Each dressed in white overalls with matching hard hats and the harsh contrast of an M16 rifle slung tight over their shoulders.

Three of their number busied in and out of the building as the remaining pair manhandled valves at the back of the tanker parked alongside.

Adrenaline surged from my core when I saw there were no hoses connected to the wide outlets they were rushing to open.

Clear liquid soon poured from the truck's wide outlet, vapour shimmering the yellow warning signs covering its bulbous rear.

I hesitated, unmoving when I should have been doing anything but watching with disbelief as the hazy liquid blackened the dusty tarmac and made its way at a rising pace towards the drains and building where I stood; the building where the poor victims still lay.

Picking up my feet to move, I stopped for a second time with my stare fixing through the wide doors at the base of the chimney, all at once grateful I didn't have binoculars.

I didn't want more detail of the lifeless white forms, some limbless and bloodied, piled just inside.

Pulling up the Glock, I took aim at the nozzle; a difficult shot at this range, but not impossible.

Putting pressure on the trigger, I took a deep breath, but paused as movement caught in the left corner of my vision.

Turning towards a second Jeep, this time in white, I let the gun drop as I made out Frank through the passenger window. With windows in the back blacked out, I could only guess it would be Ally driving.

Its horn blared and I watched hands raise at the tanker, beckoning them past.

I took up the gun again, set the silver nozzle in the sight, lifting just a little to account for the distance.

The round pinged against the metal and reflex had me turning, my arm covering my face as I felt the flash of heat sending my senses crazy. The sound came next, the great suck of air as the flames consumed its surroundings to satisfy its great appetite.

No explosion followed and I turned back to see the road alight, as were the five men darting around the burning tarmac.

The explosion came to cut down the five men as they tried to rush from their fate, but it was the dark Jeep's fuel tank which had caught, forcing the tanker towards the chimney.

Crouching, I hesitated with my fingers in my ears, waiting for the building to shake. I stood tall when the earth beneath me didn't quake and took in the tanker, still intact despite the jagged cuts and dark metal shrapnel sticking out from its sides.

With the liquid on the road almost used up and the fire dimming, only a bright white flame from the nozzle remained like an upturned blow torch directed at the base of the chimney.

The remaining Jeep built its speed as the driver recovered from the shock of the explosion and it looked like they were going to attempt to rush past the burning tanker, rolling over the boiled, blistering tarmac.

A bold or stupid move, I couldn't quite decide. Either way they were moving forward and passing beyond the edge of the building.

I fired off shots which should have been easy, but seven rounds later I'd only shredded the rubber on the two nearest tyres, having little effect to their building motion.

I swapped out the magazine, running backwards to get the angle and emptying the Glock into the rear left as it presented itself.

Still, with only one tyre remaining they continued, the

211

engine roaring, the metal rims grinding to churn the tarmac. But now with just one wheel remaining, the steering had jammed left, the drag too much even for the steering servos to correct. With so little rubber on the road, the brakes were useless and they had no way to avoid the trees at the edge of the car park they raced toward.

With a grind of metal and a shower of leaves, they came to rest with loose branches raining down as steam hissed from under the hood.

Abandoning the Glock, I shot a glance back to the stairs, then to the Jeep and peered down the vertical face at my feet. My survey soon caught on a drainpipe. Turning around, I lowered over the edge.

Crunching to the gravel, I pushed the Ruger out in front, watching the doors of the Jeep for signs of movement as I ran.

My thoughts turned to the ease of my victory and an end to this job which had turned out so grim. I could take what remained of my target, get on with another chapter and do my best to forget the sorry set of firsts.

I saw the white of airbags before anything else, then the empty pair of seats. The passenger door hung open a crack and I just about saw a pair of feet and her thin ankles in the distance between the dense trees.

I ran across the front of the car, heat pluming towards me as I turned to the red-hot bricks, the flame still intense from the tanker's back. I couldn't help but glance up the length of the chimney for a moment before racing off on the chase.

With no path to follow, their going was slow through the dense undergrowth; mine the easier task as their fight had pushed the branches and thorns out of the way, but still their only sign was the occasional shred of clothing hanging on a thick branch.

However, soon the brambles cleared and the chase switched to a well-trodden dirt path and I had sight of Ally's back.

She wore a short lumberjack shirt over the tee I'd seen her in when they'd left me to be defiled and then killed.

Frank ran a few paces ahead, limping on his right foot.

Their voices were faint but I could hear the strain in his; hers calmer, more like they were chatting over drinks.

I watched as Frank took a left and I sped, following Ally around the curve of the path. They were looping back, realising their best chance would be another vehicle from the compound, if only they could stop me catching up.

I should have stopped and taken aim. I could have so easily. Instead, I watched as Ally glanced back for the first time; watched as her eyes grew wide and as she stumbled at my sight.

I watched as she slowed, stopped and turned, only glancing once behind her to make sure Frank limped out of sight.

As she turned, I saw the boxy shape of a firearm at the top of her leggings, the rest covered with the loose check shirt. I kept the Ruger raised as I met her eyes, the surprise still hanging on her brow.

I searched her features and read surprise. Intrigue, perhaps. But was the happiness I saw real? A smile rose from the corner of her mouth.

Still, I hadn't gone completely mad; hadn't left sense and my training on the roof. I knew I couldn't trust myself. I was far too close to this now.

I had, after all, been in love. I still just might be. However, I couldn't help but smile with the gun still raised in her direction as I stopped just outside of her reach.

"Hey, Cat," she said with a longing in my direction, her voice softer than I'd expected.

"Hey, Ally."

"This you?" she said, looking in the rough direction the path headed toward.

I gave a slow nod.

"Frank was right about you," she said, her white teeth glaring towards me.

"How?" I asked. Of course I didn't care, but I hung on her words nonetheless.

"You've got amazing skills. You could be great with us. You could flourish," she said, raising her eyebrows. "And I'm sorry."

"For what in particular?" I asked, trying to take my eyes from her face and make it look like I was more concerned about Frank's location when in reality I'd almost forgotten about him.

"For underestimating you," she replied.

I could feel my eyes welling, the emotion ready to boil; anger, pain and something else I dared not put a name to.

"Do you love me?" I said, the words sounding so feeble, my chest tightening as I directed my anger inward.

"I do," she said, her eyes wide and mouth drifting open. The pain released.

"I love you, too," I replied and bit down on my lip. My arms dropped, the Ruger pointing to the ground. I tasted blood.

"I'm sorry for not bringing you in earlier. I'm sorry for falling for you."

"So why did you leave me to die? Why did you leave me to be raped and killed at the hands of those three?"

Ally laughed as if I'd told a corny joke. "I knew you could handle them. I'd seen you in action, remember?"

I couldn't reply. Doubt clawed at my mind. She was right after all; I had handled all three.

"So why were you so surprised to see me?"

"I thought you'd run. I thought you'd get out. Why come for him? For me?" she said, tilting her head to the side. "But I'm glad you did. Come with us," she said, outstretching her hand.

I took a step towards her and let the grip of my right fall from the Ruger. I moved my hand up. I moved to touch her, but just as I felt her warmth I took a step back, clasped my fingers back around the gun.

"I don't want to be a part of this," I said, shaking my

head, a tear rolling from my eye.

"You think I do?" she replied.

I kept quiet.

"Do you think I want to be involved?"

I said nothing. I felt my mind putting up barriers my heart was all too willing to let her climb.

"What he's doing here is disgusting. Barbaric. Inhuman." She paused and I felt the barriers fall. "Is that what you want me to say?"

I kept quiet as my chest tightened.

"You're right," she said. "It's a tough price to pay. These people are heroes. These people are paying to stop others suffering."

"Did they volunteer?" I said, stopping her words. It was her turn to pause.

"Of sorts."

"Did they volunteer to be Guinea Pigs? Did they volunteer for the torture in the name of progress?"

"Not in so many words. It's not too late," she said. "Come with us. We'd make a formidable force."

"I've heard that before," I said, letting a smile rise at the memory. "Anyway, I can't. I don't want to be with him."

"We come as a package. We come with all this," she said.

I shook my head, my teeth in my bottom lip.

"So what are you going to do?"

"I have my orders," I said under my breath.

"What are your orders?" she said, brushing off my words with a grin.

"I have to bring Frank in."

"What are they going to do to him? Will he stand trial?" she said as a laugh bubbled from her chest.

"I'm not the police."

She looked a little surprised at the words.

"Bureau?" she replied.

I shook my head.

"Private? From the families?"

"You'll never guess."

"Who then?"

"I work for a badass group of people that won't tolerate mass-murder for any cause."

She paused as if trying to judge if I was making this all up. "How noble," she finally said, raising her eyebrows. "And what are your plans for me?" she replied, letting the right-hand corner of her mouth drift open.

Mine mirrored her expression without my command. "You have two choices. I disobey my command and you can come with us. Or I have to eliminate you."

"You couldn't," she said, rearing back.

"Your choice," I said, raising the Ruger.

"You couldn't, Cat," she said, turning.

I thought of the body parts strewn at the base of the chimney. I raised the gun and pulled the trigger.

44

I knew the gun wouldn't fire.

I knew with only an unreasonable doubt the gun was too dirty, too full of lint for the striker to connect and explode the charge the other side of the metal.

I knew there was a chance it would fire. I'd let the fates decide, and they had.

She was coming with me, if she liked it or not. Although I had to catch her first and she was fast. I watched the muscles in her legs working as I pumped my own, pushing off harder with every step. I felt myself gaining, but only a fraction and I could see the light from the compound for the first time as the path took a turn.

With each step the path widened, opened out, the brick of the building there and then not, all of a sudden blocked by the white of a Jeep lurching to a stop.

Frank jumped out, limping around to the rear passenger door and pulling it open. He then ran back around to the driver's seat, pushing his foot and forcing the revs high.

She sped at his sight.

I gave it everything I could and somehow I closed the distance, catching faster, the whites of his eyes spurring me on.

Just out of touching distance, I threw the useless Ruger at her feet and it was enough to sway her off balance and she stumbled, tripping over, her knees digging deep into the mud and leaves as she skid.

I lunged at her back, but turned just as the momentum had bled off and ended up planted across her hips, my hands battering hers away from the Glock still tucked in her waistband.

I heard the car door open, glanced to see Frank pulling from his seat and felt her fist hard against my left cheek.

"I've got this," she shouted, but not for my benefit.

I chanced a look up and another blow glanced at my face.

Frank stood, lingering at the car, glaring at me with such a hatred as I'd ever seen.

A third blow landed to my cheek, this time enough to take my balance and I was the one underneath.

Her hands pinned my wrists above my head. She huffed and puffed her breath and moved to look at Frank.

"I've got this," she said, slower this time, letting her breath catch.

She turned back, her face close as she held my arms firm.

I didn't struggle.

She leant forward, her sweet breath washing over me, her lungs still running hard. "We were meant to be like this," she said, leaning closer still, letting her body rest on mine, her warmth soaking into me. Her lips so close.

My head had formed a scab over my heart and I wouldn't let her pull it off, even though it had barely set. I knew if she did, it would make the pain all the worse.

I closed my eyes and let the words slip. "I'm sorry," I said and rocketed my forehead straight into the bridge of her nose.

The release was instant, her hands jumping to her face. I turned her over, jumped up, looked to the car. I could see Frank deciding, the engine revving hard as his view switched between us and the way of his escape, past the chimney.

The shot rang out louder than I expected.

I was down, flat on my back before I knew it, my head smashed against something hard with Ally's shadow standing over me, fixed with a fierce expression; her nose out of shape, flattened at the top, blood dripping as she scowled down the barrel of the Glock as I blacked out.

45

My energy had gone.

My right shoulder stung as if consumed with flames. I couldn't see her anywhere.

I was too late, but then again I wasn't dead.

She hadn't killed me. Why hadn't she taken the chance?

The rev of an engine pulled me from my thoughts and I bent my neck to turn my head upward. The sides of my vision darkened as I did.

There she was, running backwards with a smile on her face as she saw me lift, a kiss blown in my direction with a spray of blood. She turned and ran to the car with her left hand at her nose, the Glock still in her right.

I sat up, retching, but nothing came up.

The Ruger lay at my feet. I picked it up and turned, pulling back the slide and letting the round fly from the chamber as I tried to put one foot in front of the other.

Taking a deep breath, I blew hard into the barrel, almost passing out. They saw me coming and the engine revved high. She was in the back of the car and shouting, but the sound dulled as the door slammed closed.

The car kangarooed, jumping forward, then abruptly stopped.

I smiled. He hadn't driven in years. An act of love in those first few. Or an act of guilt.

No matter now, the Jeep had gone from my vision. I ran on, the path more uneven at my feet than I remembered, but I made it to the end. Made it to the compound.

The Jeep built up speed and I listened as the gears crunched. The tyres swerved this way and that around each obstacle; tar lifted from the liquid road.

My gaze drifted left to the white-hot bricks at the base of the chimney, the tanker's flame still in full flow. A smile rose as a thought came to mind and I swapped the pistol to my left hand, my shoulder too painful on my right.

I levelled the sights at a dent in the tanker's curved

white side and waited.

I waited for the SUV to pass clear of the cylinder, then pulled the trigger. The round exploding from the chamber was nothing compared to the violence of what happened next.

As the tanker blew, it knocked me to my ass, shrapnel pinging across every surface.

When I dared to look as the projectiles settled, I watched the brick chimney fall away from me in slow motion. I couldn't watch and lay back down, not moving until I heard the mighty structure hit the ground.

***

The dust settled with each of my slow steps.

At first I saw the bricks strewn across the blacktop, some crushed, some whole, some unrecognisable as having been part of something hundreds of people had looked on every day.

Varying my path to avoid the rubble, I pushed my mouth into the crook of my arm. I had no stomach for breathing in the remains of Frank's victims.

As I drew closer to where the top of the stack landed, I heard the first sound. The slow, pained moan in what remained of the SUV. The front half anyway.

The bonnet sat raised at an angle, its white paint gone, each surface caked in black ash. The ash of his victims.

The back of the Jeep was no longer there; everything behind the driver's seat flattened beyond recognition.

I was thankful for the soot covering Ally's pulverised remains leeching to the tarmac.

46

With the air rushing through the windows, I slowed the Viper, taking the exit from the three-lane. My shoulder stung as I took the turn; with more damage to my coat it was little more than a flesh wound, but still hurt like hell even after the long drive.

For the second time in just a few short days, it was my skull that had taken the brunt, the bullet making me stumble back, causing me to fall and smash my head. I would remember that one for the future.

I'd be more careful next time. I'd be more careful with my feelings, more careful with my head. I'd remember not to mix business with pleasure and remember not to trust a pretty woman in a short skirt. Another lesson learned and something I'd keep with me for the rest of my career.

Taking the anonymous turn to the right, I rolled along the dusty road into the low commercial district with its small units and tall metal warehouses.

I watched addresses pass left, pass right, turning again as I found the one they'd given me once I'd made my second call.

Letting the V8 idle, I pulled up to the roller shutters, waiting as they rose high enough for me to pass. The engine growled as the metal closed behind me and I drew up to the intercom rising from the ground on a thin pedestal.

The engine purred as I pressed the call button and responded to the question.

"Agent Carrie Harris with a delivery. He's going to need putting back together."

GJ
STEVENS
AN
AGENT CARRIE HARRIS
ACTION THRILLER
THE
GEMINI
ASSIGNMENT

Only hours after stepping from a plane, and still reeling from the turmoil of her last assignment (LESSON LEARNED), Agent Carrie Harris's journey to headquarters is interrupted when the Operation Centre task her to hunt down something so sensitive they can't even tell *her* about it.

Carrie is under no illusion that her second official assignment would be easy, but little did she know, whilst hunting down the first clue, a childhood she'd consigned to a distant memory would confront her in a way only helpful to the enemy.

Distracted by a time she'd thought she'd forgotten, Agent Harris battles to concentrate on the hunt leading her across London and onwards to the suburbs, hoping to stay one step ahead of rivals intent on getting to the prize first.

Despite a constant concern that if she doesn't succeed so many could die, including an innocent who'd become so important to her, the chase takes her over the ocean where her fears seem as if they have come true. Can our hero stay focused enough to see if she's a match for the evil she's confronted with and return what was stolen, or will Carrie lose everything she holds dear, including her life?

Liked what you read?

Please leave a review on the platform you used for the purchase or **www.goodreads.com**. Honest reviews are difficult to come by and are so important to indie authors like me.

Visit **www.gjstevens.com for news about new releases and sign up to the mailing list to receive free books!**

www.gjstevens.com

Other Books by GJ Stevens

Agent Carrie Harris Action Thrillers

OPERATION DAWN WOLF
CAPITAL ACTION
THE GEMINI ASSIGNMENT

James Fisher Series

FATE'S AMBITION

Post-apocalyptic Thrillers

IN THE END
BEFORE THE END
AFTER THE END
BEGINNING OF THE END

SURVIVOR – Your Guide to Surviving the Apocalypse

Printed in Great Britain
by Amazon

70536912R00139